QU1NT1N'S MAN

David Rees

QU1NT

1N'S MAN

ELSEVIER / NELSON BOOKS
New York

First published in the U.S.A. (1979) by Elsevier/Nelson Books, a division of Elsevier-Dutton Publishing Company, Inc., New York. Published simultaneously in Don Mills, Ontario, by Thomas Nelson and Sons (Canada) Limited.

Copyright © 1976 by David Rees

Library of Congress Cataloging in Publication Data

Rees, David, 1936-
  Quintin's man.

  SUMMARY: Eighteen-year-old Luke has a desperate
longing for Cheryl but everything seems to stand between
them.
  I. Title.
PZ4.R32880i 1978   [PR6068.E368]   823'.9'14   [Fic]
ISBN 0-8407-6593-2   78-26308

Printed in the U.S.A.   First Edition
10 9 8 7 6 5 4 3 2 1

QUINTIN'S MAN

One

UKE opened his eyes. The dream was now only a confusion of fragments: music he thought he had composed himself, but it was not; his mother watching him; Cheryl running along an endless corridor. "I only wanted to start a conversation with you!" His own words had awakened him.

It was unusually quiet; there was not a sound from the road outside. The light was stronger than it should have been, it had a curious hard quality. He wondered if he was still dreaming.

His father came in with a cup of tea.

"I'm sorry, Dad. It was my turn."

"It's all right. I couldn't sleep. How's lover boy?"

"Condition not so good."

"Oh?" He smiled faintly.

"No. I'm fine."

"I saw you late yesterday afternoon. Following her through the arcade you were. Again." He shook his head. "Why don't you find someone else, son?"

"I can easily do that. There's plenty of girls."

"But it must be her?"

"Yes."

"It's snowed in the night." He put the cup down on the table. Luke got out of bed and lifted the curtain. "Don't stand by the window like that! People will see you!"

"It's only a body."

"I don't know what to do about you. What will the woman opposite us think?"

"She'll need a telescope to see through the frost on this window. Brrrrh! It's freezing!"

"Put some clothes on then." Luke picked up his jeans. "What are you doing today?"

"Doing? Ah, yes, I'd forgotten. Vacation. I don't know. I ought to write an essay."

"I'm going in to wash up." His father moved to the door. "You're excused for breakfast today. Angie's here."

"I'd forgotten that too. How long are they staying?"

"I don't know. Ask Adam. Sunday or Monday. He said something about classes, nine o'clock some morning or other. I can't remember."

"Long drive, Manchester. She must be special, this one, bringing her all this way."

"Hmm. Nice having a woman to cook for us, though."

"You and me do all right."

"All the meals. All the cleaning. They're not jobs for

a man." He left. Now that Adam was at the university, Luke and his father lived alone. Mrs. Edwards had died of cancer three years before, when Luke was fifteen.

He rubbed the mist on the window. Big furry flakes were still falling, some of them touched the glass and congealed to frost. The hedges of the gardens opposite were weighted down with snow, their twigs and branches, bearing heavy white heads, hanging. The plowed field at the end had been ironed out flat; nothing, it seemed, had ever disturbed its surface. In the road itself were the gray cat's-cradle lines of a car that had done a three-point turn, and drainage pipes, left at the side by men working on the sewage system, were draped with a sheet like legs in bed. Above the roofs of the town rose the steep north side of Dartmoor, like a huge woolly cloud.

Downstairs in the kitchen Dad was cooking breakfast.

"Where's Angie then?"

"They're still in bed."

Luke yawned and stretched. "You were twenty years old once."

"You don't have to remind me. I enjoyed my life till your mother was taken ill. Too much, I'm thinking, for comfort."

Luke recognized the mood. Sometimes there were, even now, days of blank depression; then Dad would go out for an evening and drink himself senseless. Luke had learned not to cross him at these times. He suffered too, for he longed to help, but his father just wanted to be left alone.

"Tell me about it, Dad."

"No. You get on and enjoy your own life." He cracked another egg into the frying pan.

Luke went into the sitting room and turned on the record player—Vivaldi's *Four Seasons,* the Winter Concerto, first movement. Adam put his head around the door. His face was bleary and unshaven. Luke, six foot one, was taller than his brother and dark-haired; Adam was red-haired, less physical an animal. Adam was also less intellectually gifted, but he didn't resent this. They were the closest of friends.

"Not that bloody thing again," he said. Luke made a rude gesture. "Still, appropriate, I suppose."

"Why?"

"Winter, isn't it?"

But it was late summer that Luke was thinking of. He had been alone, in the music room at school, listening to this, when she had walked in. He had known Cheryl vaguely for most of his life. In his small country town most young people of the same age had known each other nearly all their lives. She was looking for Miss Wharam, the music teacher. Some errand he couldn't now recall. They talked for a minute perhaps. It seemed to change his existence. Girls had been in his life since he was fifteen; he was lucky in his looks, the sort of boy girls usually want to be seen with. Nothing had ever been very serious—it was mostly the interest of finding out how far the other was prepared to go. This was quite different. But she wouldn't go out with him. There was a boyfriend already—Tony, a year older than him, who had left school as soon as he could, a slow, well-built boy who had gone straight to work on his father's farm.

Luke followed her around. He watched her in the swimming pool. He took photographs of her when he thought she wasn't looking. It only annoyed her, as he knew it would, but he couldn't help himself. Once, in class, he found he was quite by accident sitting next to her. He wrote on her desk lid: "I only wanted to start a conversation with you," but she scribbled over it furiously with a red felt pen. Fortunately old Mr. Masters, who taught them World Problems, was elderly and near-sighted, and very enthusiastic about terrorism.

Vivaldi's elaborate tone pictures Luke thought silly: a winter morning walk, people slipping on the ice and falling on their bottoms and all that. Underneath it was energy locked up, trying rather desperately—like him—to break out. Poor Vivaldi never made it, not in this piece, anyway. He was all hemmed in by the elegant conventions of the period. There it was, a nagging ticking insistent heartbeat, edgy nervous discords, the violin more fluid, trying to escape, never succeeding. Then came a comic part, like gigantic scrubbing brushes scraping each other, and it was over. He replaced it with the Bach *Fantasia and Fugue* in C Minor. This was on a grander scale, but essentially the same. The power of the organ should bring the cathedral crashing down, but it never would. Nothing was released as the self, he knew, could be released for a moment, or as love should release it, not for ever, but longer than a mere moment. There was one place where it almost happened, a passage where the organ pedals were a crouching tiger, playing grandmother's footsteps with God, but it passed without climax, dissipated in the ordered world of fugues and church architecture—God reduced to a set of musical doctrines.

The door opened. "Oi, Semprini!" his father shouted over the noise. "George Thalban Ball! André Previn! Go and eat your breakfast! I'm off to work."

Adam must have told him all those names, Luke thought. His father shut the front door and walked out into the snow. He was the foreman of the municipal road gang; they would be shoveling snow all day. Luke turned the record player off. He was going to succeed, more than his father. More than Vivaldi. Bach? Well, that *was* a big name, certainly. He had a place at Sussex University to study English if he passed his final exams this summer; after that . . . he did not know. But whatever it was, he was going to do it *well;* the energy in him wasn't going to remain locked up forever. There was a future for him, as he always knew, knew for a certainty, whenever he climbed out of the dark little town and up onto the wide spaces of the Dartmoor wilderness.

But she was holding him back, stopping him from the next stage, the real relationship, and all that energy was futile and turned back inside himself. She was preventing him from maturing.

Adam was eating a fried egg. "Yours is cold and revolting," he said.

"Angie still in bed?"

"Yes."

"What's she like?"

Adam misinterpreted. "Why the hell should I tell you?" He looked annoyed.

"No, no. I meant . . . well . . . are you in love? Both of you?"

Adam nodded. "Yes. We are." He smiled.

"What luck. What luck."

Adam looked at him, surprised by the emotion behind his words. "Be patient," he said. "Are you coming to this party tonight?"

"Owen Crawley's? You bet."

"It will be the same party we've been to all our lives." Owen, who was in the senior class with Luke, was celebrating his eighteenth birthday. "We're going for a short while."

"No need to sound so blasé. A party's a party. Usually worth it, whoever's there."

"I'm not looking for women or dope, and I don't particularly want to get drunk."

"Talk to old friends."

"We've probably all outgrown each other."

"Stay with Dad then. He's depressed again, I think."

"I noticed."

There was no need to talk about this; they both knew the problem inside out. They would lead lives very unlike their father's, they knew this. They'd probably be a long way away, with more money, different relationships, other values, growing always further from the source. It was the fault of education. The pattern could not be changed now, and their father in any case would be distressed at their attempting anything other than what they needed to be. But it made them both feel guilty, it wasn't right—Adam and Luke were aware of that.

"I'm going out in a moment," said Luke. "So you can have the place to yourselves."

"Where to?"

"The Tartan." It was a café in the center of town. "Some of the kids will be there, I guess."

"She will be, you hope."

"She sometimes goes in there, yes."

Adam smiled. "Nothing I can say, is there?"

"No. Are you using your car this morning?" It was a small compact, ten years old, with an overly loud exhaust box, repainted several times, now a mixture of black and purple. Adam frowned. "Adam! You've never refused. I've had plenty of practice since I passed the test. That was over a year ago!"

, "It's not that. I trust you. Anyway the car's so old it wouldn't matter that much if it were written off. But . . . look at the conditions."

"I won't go haywire just because of a little snow. You're an old woman."

"What time will you be back?"

"I don't know. Lunch time, one o'clock. I'll knock loudly."

"Some nerve!"

Luke leaned on the counter trying to make his coffee last. It was a dismal place when no one he knew was there to bring it to life. Tony was there, it was true, but Luke didn't know him very well, and in the present circumstances he certainly did not want to talk to him. Perhaps he was waiting for her. It was worth staying, just in case. Tony was playing the pinball machine with three youths Luke had not seen before. Otherwise the place was deserted. There were empty tables and chairs, a dirty counter, the coffee machine, peeling walls. The jukebox blared. A roll sat in a plastic case, with ham curling at its edges. Everything was cheap and unpleasant. Outside, shoppers hurried, their heads down against the snow. It was not frozen here on High Street, but the sidewalks were wet and there was the noise of the traffic in the slush.

The door opened. His heart turned over. There was snow on her coat and her hair. Her face was flushed and her eyes sparkled with the cold. She looked at him a second, giving him no sign of recognition.

"Tony! I'm so glad I've found you!"

"Why? What's wrong?"

Luke stirred his coffee.

"One of the horses has broken loose. It's out on the moor somewhere." Cheryl lived on a farm, huddled up against the edge of Dartmoor. "Can you help me? Mum's busy in the house, and Dad's gone to Exeter. He's just dropped me at the corner. There's no one else."

"No, my sweet, I can't. I'm waiting for my dad, then we're going back home."

It was the chance of a lifetime. "I'll come," said Luke. He finished his coffee. "What are you waiting for?"

"Well . . ." Cheryl looked at Tony, but he said nothing. She stood there, looking from him to Luke.

"I've got the car," said Luke. "We won't be long."

"I don't know if I ought." She looked worried. "I wouldn't bother you, but the horse is young, and . . ."

"There's my dad," said Tony, waving to someone out in the street. "I'm sorry, Cheryl. I just can't come up now. We're too busy on the farm. I'll see you tonight."

"Maybe."

He took a step toward her. "Now listen. I'd come if I could. I mean it."

"Tony, I can't bring her in on my own. I—"

"Luke will do it for you. He's big and strong. Aren't you, Luke?"

"Come on," said Luke, pulling at Cheryl's sleeve.

"You," said Tony, pointing at Luke. "Watch it."

"What for?"

"Just watch it."

"Tony, don't be so silly!" said Cheryl. "He's only going to help me find the horse!"

"When he's done that, send him home. I'm sick and tired of him following you about all over the place. I'll see you this evening, Cheryl."

Luke drove back home and, leaving Cheryl outside in the car, he went indoors to change from shoes into walking boots. There was no sign of Adam and Angie. He went upstairs and opened drawers, looking for a compass and an old woolen helmet that would keep the snow off his head. A murmur of conversation came from the next room. There, on the other side of the wall, were his brother and the girl who was really important to him. He thought of his earliest memories of Adam, a kid of five, running around the garden with his friends; Adam with a badly cut knee, howling in pain, running to their mother—Mum, large, comfortable, soothing. Now Adam was a man—he might even marry this girl, start where their parents had started. Where had the time gone? It was a strange sort of miracle that allowed a kid so high to change into a man, slipping into it almost unnoticed. It was a marvelous mysterious process. Mum. Luke pushed that picture out of his head. Even after all this time, it was the one thing that it was not possible to explain, a nasty unhealed bruise. Nothing would ever smash him up again; he was determined about that.

He turned the car out of the High Street, and drove up the hill to the moor. The last houses sank below them. The road was still fairly easy, though the snow was thick at the sides. The hedges without their greenery were skeletons of dark twigs, and the army camp, crouching under Rough Tor, looked bleak and inhospitable. He stopped the car and Cheryl opened the gate onto the moor. He drove on slowly, through the stream. She ran after him, over the little footbridge, slipping in the snow.

"My God, it's cold!" she said. "That poor horse!"

"We'll find him. Don't worry."

"Her."

Now the driving was difficult. The slowest speed was in the lowest-possible gear, he remembered, but even so the wheels slithered and spun, and it was not easy to steer a straight path.

"You should have chains," she said. "Dad has."

"It's Adam's car. He'd have a fit if he knew it was up here. You remember him, my brother?"

"Yes, I remember Adam. Very well."

"Very well?"

"I went out with him once or twice. When I was fifteen."

"Did you? I never knew that."

She looked out of the window, not answering. At first sight the snow here seemed pure and untouched for miles, apart from lines that flurries of wind had caused. It was not so virgin on closer inspection, Luke thought. Tiny arrow patterns of birds' feet were printed on it in places, and, as the wind eddied, snow toppled from dead heather into trails of white sparks. The windshield wipers swished back and forth. The flakes driving at the glass in a distracting pattern hurt his eyes.

"Adam and Luke. Odd names for—"

"For my background, for my type of family?"

"No. All right, yes."

"Luke's an old family name. Adam was Mum's choice, though why, God knows."

"No need to drive into the farm. Her tracks go toward Quintin's Man. Drive on a bit." They passed the farm, a dark shape below to the left. There was a small fir grove at the edge of its land, the last sign of human encroachment onto the wilderness, a black square on the prevailing white. The car skidded a little. This road, a military road, was a loop. It climbed up to nearly two thousand feet, then turned on itself, following another valley back to the army camp. Luke drove as far off the road as he dared, where he remembered a track started, and switched off the engine. He slid his arm along the back of her seat.

"We've come to look for a horse," she reminded him.

"In a minute."

"You just don't know how to behave. Unlike your brother."

She got out of the car. He did so too, slamming the door. The ensuing silence and the smothering of everything suggested they could be the last people left alive. The only sound was the sound of the snow itself, soft and muffling, as the wind blew flakes against the ground. Luke put out his tongue, and the little white stars pricked it with chill needle points. It would stop soon. Already the outline of the hills around was beginning to emerge—Yes Tor, and the highest tip of southern England, High Willhays, then Great Kneeset, Hangingstone Hill, and Steeperton Tor. The raised points formed a continuous irregular line that stretched around them in an almost unbroken circle. Some, like Yes Tor, had on their peaks great outcrops of rock and piles of broken granite, known as clitters, where the land had eroded—the peculiar and original mark of this landscape. Beyond the circle of mountains was a different shape, the smooth curving breast of Cawsand; beneath it the Exeter road, and, beyond, the civilized farms, fields, and neat thatched villages of the mid-Devon plain.

"The highest point in the world," said Luke. "Up here I feel free. Climbing away from the town is like shedding old skins."

"My mother loves coming up here to paint," said Cheryl. "But it's not much of a living for farmers."

Luke pulled himself together. "Now, where's this horse?"

They trudged along the track up Hangingstone Hill, treading the snow into the ground as they went. It was about a foot deep on the average, deeper in potholes, but never too severe, for there had been insufficient wind to drift it. They had both wrapped the ends of their jeans inside their thick woolen socks, but the snow came above this and soaked through and their legs were soon wet and icy.

The snow stopped falling quite suddenly. A moment later there was watery sunshine, enough to make the white land dazzle with a million diamonds. Luke put on his sunglasses. With these and his woolen helmet there was little of his face visible.

"You look like a ski instructor," she said.

"We all know about ski instructors."

She smiled. "Can you see any hoofprints? I think the snow's covered them."

"May not be your horse anyway. There's hundreds of them up here." There was not one in sight. "Are you sure we're going in the right direction?"

"No, I'm not. But I think it's the most likely. There are sometimes sheltered parts under Quintin's Man and Winney's Down when it snows, and horses will go there for the grass."

"That's some way off."

She missed her footing in a pothole, but he caught her hand and stopped her falling. When she was upright, he let her go.

"It would be easier," he said, still holding his hand out. She took it. Her skin in his, even if separated by a layer of glove. . . . What marvelous dark hair she had, and dark eyes, almost black. And she was tall—he loved girls with long legs. . . . He watched their breath steam up and saw the red glow in her face, and he felt there was the same heat in his, and a similar energy driving their leg muscles forward. Already he felt the beginning of animal tiredness.

"Are you going to Owen Crawley's tonight?" he asked.

"Yes. With Tony."

"Are you very fond of him?"

"I don't see what it has to do with you."

"It hasn't, but there's no harm in asking."

"Well . . . if you want to know we're thinking of getting engaged."

He was silent, upset, then said, knowing it wouldn't help, "I'm sorry. Do your parents mind? You were only eighteen last October, like me."

"Luke. Why don't you give up?"

"I can't. One day you'll come out with me."

"I will not. Why should I anyway?"

"Because you'd enjoy it."

"You only want one thing, like all the rest of them."

"I don't. I mean, yes, I do, but that's not the point. If it were, I'd find someone else."

"You have, haven't you? What about Elaine Stephens?"

"What do you know about her?"

"She told me. Poor thing. She's half crazy about you."

"I can't help that."

"It's not right if you don't care about her."

"I don't think so. I don't see that you have to be infatuated with somebody first. If you're both happy about it, what's wrong?"

"Just like all boys. I'm sorry for her."

"What's it to do with you?"

She snatched her hand away. It started to snow again. The flakes were spiraling down in long skeins, blown on a slight breeze, and they felt wet on their eyes and lips. Its sound was a scarcely perceptible rustle, like that of ears of barley a long way off. Any tiny form of life in the roots of the grass, or darting movement in the heather, had long since been stilled. Only their legs moved, and the snow, swirling as the wind took it. Then, in the distance, a gray shape shifted, a horse, a faint noiseless movement behind driving lines of flakes, like a scratched old film.

"There she is!"

They tried to hurry, but it was not easy, and the shape dissolved into the distance.

"It could have been any horse," said Luke, stopping and staring all around. She agreed, but it was worth following. The hoofprints, however, led off the track into impossibly deep snow, where there were unknown holes and ruts and hidden clumps of heather, over which they could easily stumble and fall.

"Prince!" she shouted. "Prince!"

"Crazy name for a female horse."

"They're called mares. Prince!"

No answer. He bent down and brushed the snow from her socks and the stiffened bottoms of her jeans. "Tell me about Adam," he said.

"Nothing to tell. He was my first boyfriend."

"Did he make love to you?"

"You have some nerve!"

"Tell me."

"I was fifteen, and he was seventeen. There was nothing in it at all. He was just a nice boy to go out with."

"Adam never told me."

"Do you usually discuss these things?"

"Yes. Yes, we do. Still, I like the thought, you and Adam."

"Why?"

"Following my brother's footsteps."

"I'm not a sort of road for all and sundry to clomp their great boots on."

"I didn't mean to imply that."

"But *you've* been around, though. Elaine Stephens isn't the first."

"True. Jenny Blakey was. I was just sixteen. Then for a week there was Mary Roper, the last week of the summer term. She was two years older than me, and that made it rather exciting. She left and went off to college and I've never seen her again. So you see I've been a bit more promiscuous than you have, if it's any consolation."

"Good. And now you've told me all the details of your sex life, perhaps we can talk about something more interesting."

"Such as your pony and its whereabouts."

"It's not a pony." She stopped. "Do you know where we are?"

"Cranmere Pool's over there to our right. This is White Horse Hill, and we're going toward Quintin's

Man. I'd know it in any weather. There's scarcely a week I haven't been up here since I could walk."

In November, he recalled, the rain, warm wind, and mists had turned the moor into a morass that had tried to suck his boots off each time he had ventured up here. Then a spell of cold weather with freezing temperatures had dried up the mud and hardened the ground to concrete. The slopes ceased running in rivulets, and bogs crusted over with frost and solidified to the texture of dough; ruts dried, their edges crumbling to powder at the boot's touch, and a north wind moaned and cut cruelly. Then after Christmas it had thawed and all was soggy and soft again. Now, in February, after the charcoal-colored snow clouds had piled up in the east for days on end, winter at last had come.

"Do you know *The Four Seasons?*" He sang the tune of the Winter Concerto, and tried to walk in time to it. He remembered exactly how she had looked on that September afternoon.

"You were playing it once in the music room."

"You remember! Why?"

"Why not?"

"I'm not just a piece of furniture, then, that you ignore."

"You were looking particularly intense. It struck me. Tony never looks quite so . . . charged."

"It was you, not the music. I fell in love with you then." She was silent. "Tony wasn't very chivalrous this morning, was he?"

"Maybe not."

He was glad she knew that. He wondered how to

press this advantage, but did not quite see how. "Do you think it's worth going on?" he asked. "We're looking like snowmen, and I don't think we'll find her."

"Just a bit longer. Ooh, it's cold!"

"Come nearer."

He put his arm around her, and this time she did not refuse. The trouble was that, wonderful though this was, it made walking even more difficult. The path was becoming steeper. Patches of grass showed through the snow; dead heather and bracken protruded, damp, black, and twisted. The flakes thinned and stopped. They could see where they were. The land fell back for quite a way.

"Quintin's Man," he said. "There used to be a standing stone here. Now there's only a cairn and this mast. No red flag today."

"Or the army would have shot us to pieces an hour ago."

"It must have been about here." He was searching for a slight rise in the ground. "Look, I'm a standing stone! Quintin's man!" He stood erect, stiffly to attention.

"What did they signify, standing stones?"

"You've lived here all your life and you don't know that! It's the burial place of some important person. Me, for instance."

"You're very much alive."

"Am I? You don't really dislike me, Cheryl, do you?"

"I don't dislike you at all. At the moment."

" 'The only other sound's the sweep Of easy wind and downy flake.' " She looked at him inquiringly. "Not Jack Frost," he explained. "Robert Frost."

"Who?"

He grinned. "We haven't much in common, have we? Let's see what. Do you go to church on Sunday?"

"Not often."

"And your parents?"

"Christmas and Easter and so on. Why?"

"None of us do. Births, marriages and deaths excepted. I haven't been christened, confirmed, nor communicated."

"That's terrible."

He laughed. "And your dad owns several hundred acres and votes Conservative?"

"Not several hundred."

"My old man's Labour. What else could he be, foreman on the roads?"

"Liberal."

"Liberal!" He sounded totally contemptuous. "I suppose I'd vote Labour because he does. It's something I haven't worked out yet."

"You think you've got most things worked out, I think. I haven't."

"Sport. Now there we will have something."

"I've seen you play squash," she admitted.

"Have you? Why?"

She turned away. "It's nice to see a good game played well."

"Really!" He was intrigued. "You're sure you weren't just watching me?"

"Yes. I don't resort to things like peering through the window of a swimming pool like you do."

"But you came specially to watch me play squash."

She looked embarrassed. "Now I do dislike you."

"I like all the selfish games," he said, absently.

"I can well believe that. Luke, why are you so pleased with yourself? You'd be nicer if you weren't."

"I see a horse."

Away to their left toward Little Varracombe was a solitary horse, a chestnut, standing still in the snow. Although it was some way off they could see the spurts of breath from its nostrils. It turned its head toward them and whinnied.

"It's her! It's Prince! Prince!!" The horse began to walk toward them, and whinnied again. "She's answering! Poor thing! She must be frozen!"

"So am I."

"Do you ride?"

"No. I'd like to try, though. There's snow on your eyelashes."

"There's snow on your sunglasses. All you need is skis. Rugged."

"I need more than skis."

"Luke! But I'm grateful you helped." She squeezed his hand. He pulled her to him and kissed her very gently on the mouth.

"Come out with me." This time she said nothing. "Please."

"Why do you keep pestering me? You spoil everything." She sounded defeated rather than angry.

"If I don't persist in things I'll never get anywhere."

"If it weren't for Tony . . ."

"Forget Tony."

"No. I won't." She walked away, stumbling through the snow to Prince, who was now only a few yards off. The horse tossed its head and nuzzled against her. She

stroked its nose, patted its side. Prince looked at Luke a
moment, then shied away. "She doesn't like you,"
Cheryl said.

"I'm not bothered."

"She has no rein or halter. I hope she follows us.
Let's walk and see." They started back toward Hangingstone Hill, the horse beside them. Prince was evi-
dently pleased that her freedom was over.

"My jeans are soaked," Luke said. "And my socks."

"We can dry out at the farm."

"That will be nice."

"Don't get ideas. I'm just showing I'm properly
grateful."

"Oh, thank you very much." He was sarcastic. "You
were saying, what was it? If it weren't for Tony."

"I didn't mean it."

"You did."

"Luke. If I say something you'd like to hear, will you
please drop the subject?"

"No."

"You're very boring."

"What is it anyway?"

"You'll have to promise to drop the subject!"

"All right." He looked at his watch. "I won't mention
it for an hour." She said nothing. "Come on then. What
was it?"

"I remember how you looked at me, at school, when
you were playing that record. You see . . . I felt the
same, just a little, just for that moment."

"First reserve. First on the waiting list."

"If you like, though you make me sound horrible."

"I'll work on that." He smiled, a quiet grin of satisfaction.

"And stop looking so pleased with yourself!" He laughed, and took her hand, stopped, tried to kiss her again.

"No!"

"All right. You win. For the moment."

The sun came out. As the snow cloud receded to the west, the familiar line of peaks took shape all around them, and they became a blazing white in a sort of tribute, he thought, to his triumph. He whistled all sorts of tunes. There was no further need for conversation, though he thought of a hundred things that he could say. This afternoon he would write his essay on Edward Elgar. No, Elgar was too gloomy, full of hopelessness. If he had been one of Elgar's friends he wouldn't have been very pleased to be immortalized in those *Enigma Variations*—particularly Mr. Townshend or Mrs. Powell. Imagine having your stutter trilled out for ever by every symphony orchestra in the world! But that key change, trivial G major to E flat to start "Nimrod"; that was major, majestic, as if a door suddenly opened that had obstinately remained shut— like now. His life was going to be in E flat major, the main highway.

"What about the car?" Cheryl asked, bringing him down to earth.

"Shall I drive on ahead?"

"Perhaps you'd better follow in case she bolts. But keep well back and don't frighten her."

Prince snorted. She was very happy to be reunited

with her owner, it seemed, and did not look as if much could frighten her at all. Luke drove behind, in bottom gear, humming "Nimrod."

A big log fire roared in the open grate. The room was low-ceilinged, its beams exposed, its walls of ancient woodpaneling. There were window seats and doors with latches. It was the living room of a Devon longhouse about four hundred years old, converted to the conveniences of modern living—central heating, wall-to-wall carpet, drinks on show on a movable bar. The last century's utensils—horse brasses, a dairy-maid's yoke, fire irons—had become this century's decorations.

"Take your jeans off," Cheryl had said. "Mum won't mind."

So here he was, talking to her mother for the first time, his feet and legs bare. He was glad his shorts were clean.

"Where do you live?" she asked.

"Meath Road. In the housing development."

"Cheryl won't be long." Tony had phoned while they were out, and she was calling him back. "Would you like a beer?"

"Yes, please."

She poured it into an expensive heavy tumbler. At home he always drank it straight from the can.

"What are you going to do when you leave school?"

"I've been accepted at Sussex to study English, depending on final exams."

"Really." She sounded just slightly surprised. She wore an expensive woolen pantsuit, a little too much make-up. Like Cheryl, she was tall but thinner, with blond graying hair. She was not quite what he had expected, not the conventional middle-class farmer's wife. There was something Bohemian about her. He remembered Cheryl had said she was a painter. If they could break the barriers, he thought, they might find more in common than she imagined. She lit a cigarette, but did not offer him one. He finished his beer.

"Cheryl's taking a long time," she said.

"I'll be off when those jeans are dry."

The door opened and a large golden Labrador retriever bounded in. She made a great fuss over it, and conversation was instantly possible again—dogs, cats, other pets. Eventually she said, "I must see to things in the kitchen. Help yourself to another drink."

He did so, and sat on the hearth rug in front of the fire. It was some kind of imitation animal hair, soft and sensuous on his legs. Cheryl came in, looking very upset.

"What's the matter?"

"Tony."

He put his beer down and went over to her. "Tell me," he said, putting his arm around her.

"It's nothing." She fumbled for a handkerchief.

"He didn't like your going up on the moor with me, I suppose."

"He certainly did not. He said some very unkind things." She looked so beautiful, a tear in each eye, he wondered how he stopped himself falling with her then and there onto the hearth rug. "We're not going out tonight. That's certain."

"Did you say that?"

"No. He did." She sniffed and turned away. "He thought I'd be back when he phoned before. Then when I said you were here, in the house, he got very angry."

"Come with me to Owen's, then."

There was a long pause. "Yes, I will."

He kissed her, again very gently, then not so gently.

"Your jeans are dry, Mum said. Luke . . . I do like you."

"I love you. You know that." He let her go. "We'll call for you about eight o'clock."

"We?"

"I'll be in the car with Adam and his girl. You don't mind?"

"No. I'll be ready at eight."

As he drove back, with great care down the long slippery hill, he was elated beyond any previous imagining. He was king of the town below with its white roofs and smoking chimneys. The car behaved itself perfectly in response to his feet and hands. There was this rare sensation of everything in himself working in perfect coordination—mind, heart, bones, skin.

Adam was standing outside the front door, looking extremely annoyed. "Where the devil have you been?" he demanded. "I've been waiting for hours. Do you know what time it is?"

Luke glanced at his watch. "I'm sorry. I didn't know."

"We were going into Exeter. It isn't worth starting out now."

"You didn't say."

"Nor did you. You weren't in that café all this time, that's certain. Just look at the state of the car! You haven't been up on the moor, surely?"

"I've been helping someone look for a lost horse."

"Who?"

"Cheryl Wood. You never told me, by the way, you used to go out with her."

"Oh, I see. Getting somewhere at last." Adam followed him into the house. "You were too young then to talk to."

"Nonsense. She's the same age as me, and that didn't stop you."

"Does it bother you?"

"Not in the least." Luke grinned.

"It was all very innocent."

"I knew about things then. Spent all my time thinking about it, and talking about it, like all kids of fifteen."

"You would have told all your friends, Luke."

"Yes. I would. All right, you're forgiven." Luke helped himself to bread and cheese. "Have you eaten?"

"Yes. We'll go shopping in town, since you've stopped our going to Exeter. Is there anything to buy for dinner?"

"No. It's liver and onions and I'm the cook. You'll be in?"

"Angie will do it."

"No, she won't. Look. Dad and I have had to do all our own meals since you left home. We take it in turns, and today's my turn, and already I let him do breakfast, poor old guy. I'm quite a good cook, anyway." Adam laughed. "What's the matter?"

"You. You look like all the clichés say. Walking on air. Eyes sparkling. Ecstasy."

" 'I wonder by my troth what thou and I did till we loved. Were we not weaned till then? But sucked on country pleasures, childishly?' "

"He also said, 'Send home my long strayed eyes to me, Which (oh) too long have dwelt on thee; Yet since there they have learn'd such ill—' "

"All right, all right."

"She's not for you. Not for long. Not your type at all. I know her."

"We're calling for her at eight. She's coming to Owen's with me. 'She is all States, and all Princes, I, Nothing else is.' "

"I'll give it a week at most."

"Knock it off. And buy some wine. We're supposed to be taking a bottle."

"Anything you say. The Age of Aquarius has dawned."

Later that afternoon it began to snow again in earnest. There was a wind with it, and the road outside, from where Luke was staring at the houses opposite, was a whirling white-and-gray corridor of wool and feathers, flung downward, lifted up, driven helplessly from side to side in long horizontal lines. Gradually the shrubs and fences, the drainage pipes and roofs lost their shapes under this new accumulation. For a moment there was a pause, and Luke had a glimpse of light in the house across the road, perhaps from the fire glinting on a large copper ornament. He saw heads in a room facing the TV, then once more they were

shut out by the downpouring of gray and white dots
and zigzagging stars.

He shivered, and decided to turn on the electric fire.
They rarely used it because they couldn't afford it. He
put the Bruckner Seventh on the record player. Like
all his records it wasn't his own, but borrowed from
school. He looked out of the window again, anxious. If
it continued like this for much longer, there would be
problems in getting to Cheryl's in the car, maybe even
difficulty in driving as short a distance as to Owen's.
But here was the E Major of Bruckner's summer, the
melody that had come to him in a dream in the key of
four sharps, bright golden sunlight. It was all landscape, a slow-unfolding panorama of mountain peaks
in June or July. A few blasts interrupted the serenity,
as if some black rocky crag upreared itself against the
composer's will, but always a moment later it was blot-
ted out. This is what it will be like, Luke said to
himself—no, it's what it is now. Then there was the C-
Sharp Minor elegy, Wagner's funeral oration, not less
serene than its preceding movement despite its sad-
ness. It did not suggest a sense of loss so much as
resigned inevitability, the returning to earth of what
had come from it.

He started to compose his own funeral service. No
Christian rites, that would be absurd, in bad taste,
almost, for an unbeliever. Instead he would have the
whole of this movement played on the best quad-
rophonic equipment money could buy. Would it
sound out of place in the Exeter crematorium? And he
needed a poem. Housman's "Parta Quies," perhaps, or

"For My Funeral." And a short address, giving a considered statement of the deceased's qualities and defects. To ensure there would be no mistakes he would write it himself before he died, if given the chance. But who would be there to read it? Probably there'd be no one to mourn at all, except Adam.

As the four Wagner tubas expressed their lament— the real moment of grief when the message had come to the composer telling him of his hero's death—Luke recalled his mother's funeral, on a bright cold day in March. The clergyman had mumbled prayers in a meaningless voice, starting almost before the mourners of the previous death had left the crematorium chapel, and galloping through before the next in the line became impatient. Luke remembered the dissonance of a few relatives singing "The Lord Is My Shepherd" (her favorite hymn, Dad had said, but in fact it was the only one he could think of), and then the horrifying moment of that coffin sliding slowly but inexorably toward the furnace. He had felt numb when he and Adam and his father had faced each other afterward. He thought of the readjustment that Dad's brief words had prophesied. ("Well, sons, that's it. You two and me will start afresh.") The coffin, when the flames blasted it, did nothing happen? Nothing? He hoped it was so, fervently. When he died, out like a light, and nothing more. Let that be that. Mum.

Silence, apart from the needle scratching, brought him to the present. The music had been surprisingly upsetting, considering he had intended it simply to reflect or enhance his present state of mind. The snow still pelted outside; it seemed as if the universe had been torn into bits of paper, pouring an angry deluge over all humanity. A woman went by, doubled up, her hat almost vertical against the blizzard, her front looking like white fur from head to foot. Electric light wires sagged, resembling thick white rope.

Noticing the time, he decided to abandon Bruckner. He went upstairs and ran the hot water. He had had a bath yesterday, but tonight was going to be special. He rifled through Angie's washing things, and found a bar of deliciously scented orange soap. That would make him far more appealing than the bar of Lifebuoy he shared with Dad.

The steam wreathed up, flattened itself under the ceiling, and slowly circled the light. It had made dew on the pink-painted walls. He wrote in the moisture with one finger, "Luke loves Cheryl." He wiped it off. He stepped into the bathtub. Hot water felt different in winter. The texture of the smooth china under him was tepid, not hot, more sensuous perhaps. . . . He lapsed into his favorite bathtime fantasy: his knees protruding from the water were mountainous rocks, unscalable cliffs rising from the sea. His hair was like stones that had tumbled and splashed down when an earthquake eons ago had shaken the islands' foundations (maybe their origin was volcanic). The water between was a sea loch like those Scottish inlets that pointed right into the heart of the land, and it housed a fabulous beast of magical, legendary powers. Under the water on the lake bed of the skin were petrified forests, black bare boughs twisted now this way now that with the current, prehistoric stunted hair trees in the craters and curves of the crust that goosepimpled in the chilling water. They thinned out on the smooth swept shores of the chest ... He stood up (earthquakes, hurricanes, whirlpools) and stepped out.

While he dried himself—vigorously as after a cold swim it was so cold—fragments of his childhood floated up from the bottom of his mind: there were cracks in these walls that had always been there, for Dad never bothered to replaster but just painted over every few years, and bashes in the paint where the lavatory chain had swung (Dad was always telling him not to). These used to be steep hills in childhood, some so steep as to be more than one in one, but some a car could climb. The top gear would be dying, then third, second, and the crisis sound of first like a straining bus, passengers gaping as they looked back at the frightening view, and that sound fading, what shall we do, what's going to happen? We'll slip downward, fall off the earth, out into outer space!

He looked in the mirror. Rugged, she had said. The marks of old pimples and chicken-pox scars, more likely. Blue eyes, dark hair not quite down to his shoulders (cause of battles at school a few years back, but the staff had given up since he had been in the tenth grade, and grown their own hair longer instead). Yes, he would do for tonight. The clothes were obvious—blue brushed denims, bought just a week ago, uncomfortably tight but very flared at the bottoms, and a plain white kaftan. Now he was ready. He whirled around the kitchen frying the liver and onions, his feet dancing he felt so light with joy.

Adam and Angie arrived a moment after Dad.

"I hope none of you's going out tonight," said his father. "You'll never get back."

"The roads are still passable," said Adam. "But it will be difficult to"—Luke was making signals to him, not to say they were going up to Cheryl's; in these conditions Dad would make real objections—"I mean the Crawleys' house isn't far. Only a mile."

"Take care, then. It will freeze soon. Stay the night there if it gets worse." He pushed his cap back and scratched his head. "Terrible day. Clearing snow all morning, might as well not have bothered. Then sitting around all afternoon doing nothing. What's this then?"

Luke put a plate in front of him. "It looks to me like liver, mashed potatoes, onions and peas. It may be a mirage. I'm not sure. Don't touch it if you think it's poisoned."

"Long-haired nut!"

"I'll cook tomorrow," said Angie. "I'm sorry I didn't get up in time for breakfast. I'll do all the meals."

"Somebody will have to," said Dad. "It's Saturday. I shan't be up."

"What are you doing tonight, Dad?" Luke asked.

"Might go down the pub later if the snow holds off."

"Might! Have you ever missed a Friday?"

"I don't feel that good."

"What's wrong?"

"Nothing much. You're all spruced up already, I see."

"Great developments in little brother's life," said Adam. "The most expert of lovers has persuaded the ideal of beauty to come out with him. To the party. The most passionate affair of modern times will now take place."

"Cut it out," said Luke.

"Has he now?" His father grinned. He pushed his plate back and stood up, then went into the living room and switched on the television.

"What's the matter with him?' Luke asked in surprise. "There's nothing wrong with that food. He's hardly touched it."

"He did say he wasn't well," Adam said.

"He said it was nothing much." Luke was hurt.

"If he mumbles that it's nothing much, it's probably serious. Have you ever heard him say before that he didn't feel good?"

"No. True. Do you think we ought to leave him on his own then?"

"He won't thank you for staying. He'll go down to the Exeter Arms just the same, and he'll feel obliged to take you, and he won't like that."

"Why?"

"Because he likes to talk to his friends, and his clever sons embarrass him. I mean he thinks we don't like the Exeter because we don't talk about football or gritting roads, and it cramps his style."

"It's not true. I follow football more than he does. I took him to Argyle last week. It's sad. Sad."

"I know. I love going out for a drink with my dad. I love the bloke."

"So do I." He sighed. "There's nothing we can do for him. Not anymore."

It had stopped snowing, but the weather was colder. There was a clear sky with a full moon. Icicles, rows of spikes, hung from gutters. The snow on the ground, deep and massive and soft, made the car chug uncertainly through the streets. There were few people about, and the houses seemed to have shrunk into themselves, become deadened under the weight of snow. The main road was no problem, Dad and his men having salted it, but the climb up to Dartmoor was not easy. On the bend by the railway bridge the car went into a slow skid. The wheels spun out of control, and the engine stopped. Adam allowed it to slide gently back so that it was resting against the rampart. He tried again, but it was no use. The wheels just slithered.

"I meant to bring a shovel," he said. "How far is it to the farm, Luke? I forget."

"Half a mile."

"I think you'll have to walk. I daren't go any further even if I can persuade the car up this bit. It's bound to be worse on the moor."

"I'll freeze to death."

"Trust you to come out on a night like this with nothing over that ridiculous shirt. I suppose you haven't got an undershirt on either."

"No. I don't own an undershirt."

"All you were thinking of was her, I suppose. Why the devil don't you have more sense?"

"Can I borrow your coat?"

"Oh, I suppose so," Adam took it off. It was an old navy greatcoat. "Lucky for you my boots are in the back."

"We'll be late," Luke wailed.

"Can't be helped. You push on and I'll turn the car around. We'll wait here for you."

It would be a setback, this, Luke thought, as he trudged on through the snow. First of all, keeping her waiting, and then appearing in these absurd clothes, looking quite unlike the irresistible impression he had planned to make. The scene by moonlight was much more desolate than in daytime. The blanket of snow, instead of smothering everything with a newness that was exciting, an invitation to remember all the snow games and sledding of childhood, was a dull tarnished silver in the moonlight, an unnecessary obstruction between him and his wishes. What it had promised to give that morning it was now snatching away. Thousands of stars flickered greenly in a cold sky, like eyes full of mockery.

The frost stung his ears and his toes. The wind, which had been blowing more strongly all the afternoon, moaned in the telephone wires and shook the spidery bushes, making the icicles tinkle on the twigs like bells. A row of trees, dwarfed and made grotesque by the prevailing wind direction, roared so loudly that it was impossible, he thought, that they would not fly out of the ground and crash down on his head. The army camp seemed totally deserted, a series of mysterious dark oblongs, ghost huts, out of place in the silver all around. He opened the moor gate. It was not easy now to see where the road was, for no hedge or bank separated it from the grass, and all was evenly covered. The wind kept drifting the snow, an incessant sound of whispering like dry sand as one thin layer ·shifted,

forming little markings or scribbles like dried-up
riverbeds or maps of Mars. Adam, he admitted grudg-
ingly, had been right: he could never have handled the
car in this.

There was the farm, lights in its windows. The fir
grove beyond was still black against the silver, for the
wind was too fierce to let the snow stay long on the
branches. The trees sighed like a distant sea, growing
louder as he drew near until they were an ocean un-
leashed in a storm.

Cheryl's mother opened the door.

"I'm sorry I'm so late," he explained. "The car is
stuck by the bridge and I had to walk."

"Was she expecting you?" She seemed surprised to
see him.

"Why . . . yes!"

"Well, that's very odd." She frowned. "Are you
sure?"

"Of course!"

"She went out half an hour ago. Tony came for her."
She ventured out and looked around. "It's a terrible
night. I didn't think they ought to go, but . . . young
people. Would you like to come in a moment?"

"No. No, thanks." He stumbled away, hardly noticing where he was going. The shock hit him like an
avalanche.

Two

I T was not quite the same party they had been going to all their lives, for Owen's elder brother, Jack, was there, and had brought several friends from the university with him. Luke wandered about restlessly, drinking, joining this group or that for a few moments. The party was pointless now. His house had no telephone, but surely there was some way she could have contacted him? Why? Why had Tony changed his mind? And why had she? What were they doing at this moment, this precise second?

He crossed the hall, into a room where people were dancing. The noise was deafening. So many people in such a small space; jeans and skirts; bare sleek arms of girls, bare muscular arms of boys in T-shirts. Laughter, bits of conversation, girls' faces ferociously serious. All the girls were with somebody. There had to be an attractive unattached girl somewhere. There was Elaine Stephens, with no one in attendance, but she was the last resort, a real step backward.

He went out into the hall. A crate of beer had been deposited on the landing for no accountable reason. He climbed over a couple (in an endless deep kiss) halfway up the stairs. It was Dick Allard and Suzy Benn, kids from his class at school who had been involved with each other for a long time. Why they needed to be so public, so uncomfortable, was puzzling, for they saw much of each other privately. Perhaps they needed to reassure their friends they were still together. They took no notice of him as he sat three steps above them drinking. He'd known Suzy since kindergarten, thirteen years ago. He listened to a conversation going on in the half light behind him.

"There's all sorts of edible weeds growing wild," said the first voice, male, with an American accent, "if only people would take the trouble to find out. Stinging nettles, for instance."

"But why? What's wrong with cream of tomato out of a tin?"

A long pause. "It's ethnic."

The second voice was also male. Surprised, Luke turned around. He saw a fair-haired boy with long hair; his companion was dark, with a mustache.

"Hi," said the mustache. "Don't mind us." He was the American.

"I'm sorry," said Luke. "I didn't mean to butt in."

"We're not bothering you, I hope."

"No. No. Not at all." He stood up, uncomfortably aware of their gaze.

"We are, or you wouldn't be going. Stay and talk."

"I'll be back. He clambered down over Dick and Suzy, irritably conscious that he was attracted to Suzy now that he'd seen her, and that all those years he'd never thought of it. The two men on the stairs were friends of Jack, presumably, unlikely though that seemed. There was Jack, standing by the fireplace, joking with two girls and another man. Jack was the typical English sportsman, loose-limbed, clean, blond, the best squash player the school had known, now on the university team. When he was younger Luke had played him a few times and always lost dismally.

He joined Owen and a group of friends. There was a girl here he did not recognize. She had honey-colored hair and was slim, like a Californian beach girl, and she was not with anyone in particular, it seemed.

"You can say what you like, Nic. When the barricades go up, you'll be there with your red cross and a stretcher."

"I will not. I'll be the first to start shooting."

Luke, leaning against the back of a sofa, turned to see who was sitting there. It was Adam and Angie, heads together, engrossed in a private conversation.

"Kill yourself, more like. Too drunk to know which way around the pistol is."

"Why can't you be serious for once? Ask Gary."

Gary, who had drunk a whole bottle of wine, smiled mysteriously at the girl, and she put her hand in his. Disheartened, Luke switched his attention to the talk behind him.

"I rather like the name Vernon," Adam said.

"Vernon! Ridiculous!" Angie laughed, a surprisingly musical sound. She was much more lively than she had so far appeared to be at home. Her silence there was maybe caused by Dad, who did not seem to pay much attention to her. Luke looked at her. She didn't appeal to him at all. She was a slight wispy girl with mournful brown eyes, short brown hair.

"Well, so long as it's not Julian," said Adam. "I can't bear people with the name of Julian. Or Adrian."

"These fantasies. I shall want to work for several years before even thinking about it."

Luke was impressed. People who had reached that point in a relationship must be serious. Would Adam ask him, assuming they did not consider marriage too bourgeois, to be his best man?

"Inflation makes it impossible," Adam was saying. "It wouldn't be allowed in a really civilized country."

"It isn't."

"I've been seriously thinking about it. Sun. Beaches. It's a long way, though. What about Luke?"

"No farther in the whole world. What about Luke?"

Emigrating. Why? Then he really would be alone.

"Luke! What's the matter? I've asked you twice." It was Owen. Luke came to.

"I'm sorry. Problems." He moved away, looking for more beer. The only supply seemed to be on the landing, and he didn't particularly want to involve himself with those two guys and their ethnic nettles. How annoying, they must have taken the whole case up there deliberately. In the kitchen there were several bottles of wine, and he wondered whether the best solution was to get really drunk. But he had seen his father in that state too often, and though Dad was always happy enough at the time, singing or swaying about amusingly, he always awakened the next morning with splitting headaches and a bad temper. Being drunk was no answer. There was always tomorrow. Wasn't there? He might need a clear head. He might see her. There might be some quite simple explanation. Tomorrow all might be well. And, as it might not, there must be some girl here if only he could find her, just someone to be with casually. Elaine Stephens was coming down the hall toward the kitchen. He hurried out. Anything rather than her.

"You seem out of things," said the American.

"I've been stood up," Luke said. "By a girl."

"All right. Message received." He laughed good-humoredly. "I'm Chris, and he's Paul. We won't eat you."

"You prefer nettles." Luke sat on the stairs. "I'm Luke."

"You're Luke and you don't like nettles. What else should we know?"

"Here's an interesting woman. Doesn't she appeal to you?" The beautiful girl who was with Gary was coming up the stairs. Unable to climb over Suzy and Dick, she stopped, uncertain. Luke stretched out a hand and helped her over.

"Hi, Linda," said Chris.

"So that's where all the beer, is," she said, sitting down on the step beside Luke. "I shall tell Jack. Naughty boys." She sounded maternal. Luke opened a can and passed it to her.

"How's Gary?" Paul asked.

"Drunk. As usual. One of these days I'll go home with somebody else. You, for instance."

"Why not? How about it, Chris."

"Try him," Chris said, pointing at Luke. "He thinks you're appealing." She shook her head and smiled. "More over. I was on my way to the bathroom." They shifted, and she went up the stairs, then called out from the darkness on the landing, "You've got nice long legs, though." She laughed. "Hasn't he, Chris?"

"You won't get anywhere there," said Paul. "Gary always gets drunk. And Linda never goes with anyone else."

This was all a waste of time, Luke thought. Stupid people. He took another can of beer, stepped over Dick and Suzy, and went downstairs. Adam and Angie were still in their interminable conversation, heads still together, the drink in their glasses at the same level. He stood in the doorway, watching them. The room seemed not quite real: perhaps he was now a little drunk. Across the hall in the other room were the dancers, legs bending, turning. There must be one nice girl somewhere in the crowd. It was a long fall from the afternoon to this, this sense that the party was moving on, leaving him behind.

He looked at his host. There was Owen, who had been in the same class as Luke ever since they were both eleven. Eighteen today, a bit flushed with drink, he was trying to impress Kate, another life-long acquaintance. Her desk had been next to Luke's when they were both nine, in Miss Ridgway's class; he used to bring her strawberries, stolen from a garden he passed on the way to school. All these people, still involved in a game that had started before they could even remember and he was out of it. Owen, with long straggly hair, a nose too large—Owen had always liked girls and hadn't done so badly, either. It didn't mean much. So long as people were happy. Happy, certainly, they all were, compared with him, who was of the first nothing, every dead thing. Why, Adam had once demanded in exasperation, did he have to test everything with a literary or a musical quotation? It was, he'd retorted, a reasonable yardstick, the sum of other people's tested experience. They were Mr. Mendham's, his English teacher's words, but good enough to silence Adam. Dull sublunary lovers' love (whose soul is sense) cannot admit Absence. Neither could he; nor could Donne. Donne was just pretending. It was time to interrupt. They were still there on the sofa.

"But I use your orange soap, too."

"And it makes you smell gorgeous, Adder." Yes, she used the same childhood nickname as he did.

"Hello, lover," Adam said. Luke knelt down in front of him, resting his head on his brother's knees. Adam stroked his hair.

"It hurts?" he asked.

"Yes."

"It will pass."

"Not this time."

"It will pass, just the same."

"I'm a dull sublunary lover. I can't admit absence. Have you ever been there, Adam? I mean really in love, and she's not interested? Plays with you for a morning, then goes off with somebody else?"

"No. I don't think I have."

"Then you can't know how much it hurts."

"I'll tell you something, Luke, but you won't like it. Shall I?"

"Go on."

Angie stood up. "I think I'll find another drink," she said. "Do you want one?"

"No," said Adam. "We'll talk." She went away, and Luke curled up, in a ball, beside his brother on the sofa, wishing to peel lots of both of them away and revert to childhood dependence on Big Adder.

Adam sighed. "You're very demanding, Luke."

"I tell you everything."

"You're being childish."

"I'm not. How am I childish?"

"Because you don't tell people everything. Nobody does."

"What were you going to say? Just now."

"Something about you. Do you want me to?"

"Yes."

"You always used to get in trouble at school, I remember. A long time ago I'm talking about. Annoying all the teachers. You got sent home once, didn't you? Uncontrollable, they said."

"What of it?"

"You were in court once, for stealing from Woolworth's. Thirteen you were then. Suddenly you're reformed. You decide to work, really set your mind on it. Getting straight A's. No one at school has such a record. That's what pleased you, isn't it, Luke? You decided you had to be unique. You put your considerable mind to it and did it. Is it the same with women? I

bet you were the first boy in your year to get anywhere
with a girl."

"You know I was. I've told you that before."

"Same thing, really, with Cheryl. What's the big at-
traction? She's all right, yes, no more beautiful than
half a dozen others. You haven't got much in common,
so there's only one reason. She's not available. So you
have to make yourself do what nobody else would
consider. Just another test of your big powers." Luke
stirred uneasily. "It's true, isn't it?"

"No. Not in any way."

"The most difficult conquest of all so far."

"No, Adam! No!"

"All right."

"What do you mean, all right?"

"Just putting ideas in your head. Thought it might
help to cure you."

"Cure me! Now you're being childish. Uncle Adder's
help page! Cutting me open like that. You haven't got
the right."

"When Mum died I felt as hurt for you as her. You
willed her to live, willed it and willed it. But she died."

"So what?"

"You can't bear failure, can you? I just want you to be
happy, that's all."

"So much so that you're thinking of emigrating to
Australia and leaving me here, on the other side of the
earth."

Adam stared. "You shouldn't eavesdrop."

"That's easily said. That doesn't excuse."

"You obviously didn't hear all the conversation. I did
say I wouldn't consider going if you hated the idea."

They looked at each other, and there was a moment of real dislike on Luke's part. "Luke, I mean it! I wouldn't lie about such a thing!"

"You go. I can manage. Though don't think I won't miss you, because I will." He stood up. "Can we go home soon? I'm tired."

"In a while. It isn't late."

All his feelings dissected into nasty little pieces, and it only made him want her all the more. He tried to picture her face, but it was an unfocused blur. That was supposed to be a sign of love. But, like Adam said (and did), it would be simpler to take the possible things, like Elaine. She was no worse than listening to Adam. He went into Mr. Crawley's study. There was an unpleasant smell. Three or four people were sitting about smoking. It was difficult to see because the only light was from a table lamp on a desk. Jack followed him in.

"Sean! I did say not tonight. Please. My old man will go berserk. Can't you go outside?"

"We'll open the windows in a moment," someone said.

Jack stood, undecided. There was little he could do about it. He turned to Luke. "Do you want to play squash in the morning? Owen's booked me a court at school." He pulled back the curtains and threw open the windows. "Well?"

"What time?"

"Nine o'clock. Bit early, I'm afraid."

"All right." Luke was flattered. Perhaps Jack had heard that he was now the school's best player.

"You don't sound keen." Jack was puzzled.

"Yes, I am. Sorry. I'll be there."

"Well, don't touch that stuff, you won't see the ball straight. Sean, please, when that's finished, no more."

"Okay." Jack went. Sean passed Luke the joint. He took it, though he disliked the smell and it made his heart beat uncomfortably. He didn't smoke cigarettes at all; his mother's death (the cancer had been in the lungs, and she had inhaled thirty a day for as long as he could remember) had been sufficient to stop him. Sometimes at parties he smoked a little of this sickly-sweet stuff; it usually gave him a mildly pleasant sensation, but this evening it did not. He handed it back to Sean, and left. Now it would have to be Elaine.

He went outside onto the veranda. It was snowing again, a whirlwind of flakes in the freezing darkness, like the rush of white specks in the blindness after you shut your eyes. Nothing else was visible. There should have been a spectacular view of the town, with the old ruined castle on its knoll directly below. The Crawleys' house was big, on the hill up to the moor, set back from the road behind high hedges. It must be worth a lot; Mr. Crawley was a bank manager. Luke wondered vaguely where he and his wife had gone for the evening. The wind blew snow into his face He shivered. It was bitterly cold.

"Hello, stranger." Elaine. Luke said nothing. "What's the matter?"

"You know."

"Come inside." He did not move. "Do you remember your eighteenth birthday?"

"Nothing special about it."

"You spent it with me."

"Yes. So I did." She stood by him. He put his arm around her. "Shall I take you home tonight?" Elaine nodded, pleased. "Now?"

"Mmm. I think I've had enough, yes."

He went to find Adam. "Are you ready yet?" Luke asked.

Adam looked at his watch. "Must we? I'm quite enjoying it, after all. It's only half past twelve."

"I just said I'd take Elaine home. Can I borrow the car? I won't be long."

"Give you an hour."

Luke smiled. "I'll be back."

On the doorstep Elaine said "Ssh! They may not be asleep. Take your shoes off." They crept into the hall, listening. There was no sound. In the living room he found his way in the dark; he had been there before.

She pulled his face to hers and kissed him. "What's wrong?" she asked.

"I don't know. It's no good, is it?"

"Why, Luke?"

"I don't know. Nothing's happening." He giggled, embarrassed. "This will have to stop, Elaine. I can't go on, not with someone I don't love. I could once, but I can't anymore." He stood up, fumbling with his shirt. "I'm sorry. I feel . . . it's almost as if I'd hit you, isn't it?" She didn't answer. "I can't love you."

"I know that. It hasn't mattered before. Don't go. Please, Luke."

"It's no good, Elaine." He held her hands away. 'I can't. Not anymore."

"Never?"

"I'm really sorry. I feel awful." Now he had said that,

he found he could kneel and kiss her with something like tenderness. "I'm so much in love, Elaine, I could cry. But I can't ever do that, only inside."

"I know. I love you. It's the same."

"Except that . . . I haven't with her. And I never will."

"Well . . . what is there to say?"

"Thank you. I owe you that."

"You don't. It was always beautiful, even if it meant nothing to you."

"It didn't mean nothing. I would have found someone else if it meant nothing."

"I don't suppose I'll find someone else. Not like you."

"You will."

"No." She shook her head firmly. "Never. Not another Luke."

When he returned to the party, Adam looked up in surprise. "Quick," he said. Luke snorted, and turned away, frowning. "We'll go home, then, Lu. It's not your night. Are you ready, Angie?"

Back home they were surprised to find the downstairs lights still on. It was half past one. It was very cold indoors, almost as cold as outside. They went into the living room. The television was on with only a blank screen. Dad was in his armchair, snoring. There were twelve empty Guinness bottles in various places around the room. The ashtray was overflowing, and there was beer spilled on the table.

"These don't include what he's had at the pub," said Luke, collecting the bottles.

Adam switched off the television. "We'll have to carry him upstairs. He won't come around till morning."

"Stupid old fool!" Luke exclaimed, suddenly enraged. "Let him stay there and freeze!"

"Luke! Why?"

"Because it's so pointless! Why does he have to do it?"

"He's a long way down the hill. More perhaps than we'll ever be. That's why."

"It means he doesn't love us! He's shutting us out! Shutting us out! All the time!" He raised his hands in despair.

"He tries. He really does try."

"He doesn't!"

"Come. Help me with him." Together they hoisted him up, staggering under the burden. Dad gave no sign of knowing that he was being lifted, not with a movement of his mouth nor a flicker of his eyes.

"I'll make him a hot-water bottle," said Angie.

"Do that," Adam panted, "and he'll laugh at you all day tomorrow. I don't think he's ever had such a thing in his life."

"Well, he's having one now," said Angie, firmly. "It must be freezing in that bedroom, and he isn't exactly very warm as it is. Hypothermia. You men never know what's important."

They dropped him, a dead weight, on his bed.

"You go to bed," said Luke. "I'll undress him."

"I'll give you a hand."

"No. I've done it often enough, recently."

"I can still help."

"No."

"Why?"

"I just want to, that's all." Luke undid the shoelaces and pulled off the shoes and socks. "I've just remembered, Adam. I hardly dare ask you."

"What?"

"Can I borrow the car in the morning?"

Adam groaned. "Remind me next time I come down to leave it at college! I'll thumb a lift! I've hardly seen it today. And when I have used it I've been driving around where you wanted to go!"

Luke laughed. "That's what big brothers are for."

"All right. But *don't* stay out all the morning this time. I want to go to Exeter. At two o'clock on the dot."

"I'm only going to play squash for an hour or so." Angie came in with the bottle. "Yes, I'd better set the alarm for eight."

"And put a gallon of gas in it, and don't ask me if you can borrow money from me. *You're* paying for it."

"I'll do that for you."

"Sleep well."

"I won't. See you in the morning. Good night, Angie."

The shirt and sweater were easy enough, but he gave up struggling with the undershirt. The trousers were worse, and Dad almost fell off the bed. Luke stared at his father's body. It wasn't old. Fantastic thought, that was where he came from. One tiny seed in there. What had Dad been thinking of at the time? Not him. No, not an old body. There was plenty of life still in those arms and legs. Why was he deliberately chucking it away? Only the face really showed age. It was weather beaten

from all that monotonous badly paid outdoor work.
And he had the gray hair. He bent down and kissed
him, and then, again on impulse, put his ear to his
father's heart. The beat was extremely irregular.
Something was wrong, perhaps. He wondered for a
moment whether he should call Adam. It was probably
just an excess of alcohol and tobacco. He pulled the
covers over the body and tucked them in, then went to
his own bedroom. He could have done with a hot-
water bottle himself. He curled up, again like a fetus,
under the icy white sheets. He fell asleep, thinking of
Cheryl.

There was something more satisfying about a squash
ball, Luke felt, than that used in any other game. Its
very squashiness in the hand, as if it were yielding to
the power of the person using it, was a pleasure in itself,
and even more when it was whammed by the middle of
the racket with the maximum speed his arm could give
it—faster than a stroke in tennis or badminton—and
hit exactly the right place on the wall. Thwack! And
there was pleasure in the racket itself—it was neater,
more easily wielded than the cumbersome tennis vari-
ety, or the lighter, less powerful badminton one. There
was no other game that was so absorbing, or that so
suited his talents.

Jack and he were evenly matched. Jack was more
experienced, and he saw the ball with a more consis-
tent accuracy than Luke, but Luke hit it harder and
with greater speed. This morning he was playing ex-
ceptionally well, in fact, he took all his frustrations of the
previous night out in the game. A young man sat in the

little gallery above the court, watching impassively, the only spectator.

Luke won the first two games and was a point down in the third when his concentration was interrupted by the door to the gallery opening and the sound of another person coming in to watch. It was Cheryl. He looked at her blankly for a second, then returned Jack's service, but the shock of seeing her was sufficiently unsettling for him to lose several points and the game. Jack, now very much at ease, dominated the fourth game, but the final one was even all the way, Luke's greater strength and speed winning him points as it had done at the beginning. But Jack ran out the winner, just.

They were both sweating with exhaustion. "You're the better player," Jack said. "This time next year you'll thrash me easily."

"It was a good game. I didn't like losing it."

"You won't next time. I'm as good as I'll ever be, I think. You have further to go."

Outside the door of the court Cheryl was waiting.

"I'll catch up with you," Luke said. Jack went on into the locker room. Luke leaned against the wall, fiddling with his racket. "Well?"

"I'm sorry. I don't know where to start."

"Just come down to watch a good game of squash, I suppose."

"Luke. Please—"

"I must go and have a shower, or I'll catch cold."

"I can explain everything."

"I suppose you can imagine what I felt last night. What a pleasant evening I had." He walked off.

"Luke. I'm finished with Tony. Finished. For good. That's what was happening last night."

He stopped. "You told him it was over? I don't understand." He brushed the hair out of his eyes. "And you really want . . . me?" His heart seemed to miss a beat.

"Yes."

Everything was now possible again. "What are you doing this afternoon?" he asked, dazed, wondering if it was wise to restore the situation so easily.

"I want to spend it with you. If you'll let me."

"And this evening?" His voice sounded strange to him, as if it were someone else's.

"Also. I can explain everything."

"I thought I might go to Exeter with Adam. Do you want to come? And come back to tea." He moved forward, rested his arms on her shoulders, and kissed her. "I love you," he said. "I really do love you. I know that's more true than anything ever."

"You're all sweaty."

"Is that nasty?"

"No. All salt-tasting. You."

"We'll come up after lunch. How did you get here? How did you know I was playing squash? What's all this about Tony?"

"Dad brought me down in the Land Rover. He's been scattering earth and ashes as far as the moor gate. Look at the time! He said forty minutes while he did some shopping. I've been gone over an hour!"

"But how did you know I was here?"

"We stopped at your house. Woke Adam up, I'm afraid. He told me."

"How did you know where I live?"

"I told you. I used to know Adam. I'll see you later."
She ran off.

He felt shaky, almost as if he were ill. He went into
the locker room and peeled off his shorts. The hot
water from the shower drilling down on his head and
running in rivers over his skin added to the pleasura-
ble warm shock he felt inside. Everything was now
possible again.

Jack appeared. "I must go, Luke. I've someone waiting for me."

The car soared up the hill, past the hospital where he
was born, his school, the pub where his father drank,
the motel that marked the end of town. Cheryl and he
sat in the back, holding hands. Out on the open road,
the car racing at sixty, he looked across to Spreyton
village on its ridge and the whole of Devon falling away
in squares of snow-filled fields and black nets of
hedges and leafless trees as far as the white curling
wave of far-off Exmoor, and he thought, I've never
been happier, never.

"Tell me about Tony," he whispered.

"It's finished."

"I know. But why?"

She shrugged her shoulders and sighed. "I think it
was all falling to pieces anyway. I think he was looking
for an excuse to end it somehow, and you were very
convenient, turning up like that."

"But I don't understand. Yesterday morning you
said you were thinking of getting engaged."

"Yes, I know."

"Has he got someone else?"

"I don't know. I don't think so."

"It's all very odd."

"He doesn't like you much."

"I can understand that."

"He said if I fancied you, I was a cheap bit of trash."

"He said that, did he! What else did he say?"

"He came to the house, about seven. Insisted we got things straight. I said I'd come out for half an hour. Once we were in the Fountain he wouldn't drive me back, so I walked out. But I knew you'd already have come up, and . . . well . . . he caught up with me, and I got in the car, and . . . we argued, and he told me if I was going to be so childish, it was all over. He knows that as far as you're concerned, it's more than . . . Well, he drove me home, and that was that. My evening, you see, wasn't any better than yours."

"Tell me . . . do you love me?" She looked away. He put his arm around her, his mouth against her hair. He noticed Adam's eyes in the driving mirror. "Tell me," he whispered. "We can say anything to each other now." She was silent. "Was it really just a good game of squash you liked to see?"

"No."

"What then?"

"Why must I say it? It gives you such a hold!"

"Tell me!"

"Ever since I knew you were interested in me I've fancied you. Who wouldn't!"

"Why didn't you . . . ?"

"All sorts of reasons. Tony. And being with Tony, that was easy. You . . . very difficult I think it will be.

You're so domineering, and, yes, I think quite selfish. I shan't have any existence of my own. I didn't know for ages what you wanted. Was it just sex? That made me terrified that if you left me I wouldn't be able to bear it. And I thought my parents wouldn't like you."

"That doesn't really matter."

"No, probably not. My own feelings bothered me most."

"Why, then . . . how did you come to make up your mind? You've made some sort of decision."

"Yesterday, when you were pretending to be Quintin's man. I was no nearer finding out the answers than six months ago, and suddenly I dared to think the only way was . . . well, to do something. Though in the event it all just seems to have happened. There, I swore I wouldn't tell you. Something crazy's going on in me."

"I feel exactly the same. I'm not worried about it."

"I know that too. That bothers me as well."

"Why?"

"Because I know . . . where you'll make this go."

"Will I?"

"It frightens me. Or did."

"Why?"

"Because . . . I'm not sure it ought to."

"Why?"

"I'll end up more committed than you, perhaps. And I still don't know if I should."

"I can't ask you to marry me just like that."

"No. I'm quite aware of that."

"I love you. That's enough." He pulled her closer and kissed her.

"Exeter," said Adam, loudly. "Angie and I are going

to Samuel's. What do you two want to do?" The car topped the crest of the hill, and there was the city below them. Exeter to Luke was an enchanted place. It smiled on him with promise. Where they had come from was a very ancient landscape that ended with this city. It was a gateway—on the far side, east of Exeter, was the new world, freedom and adulthood. All its young people suggested to him this kind of excitement. University students came no farther west. It was the last bastion of civilization. In more rational moments he knew this was nonsense, but all the pressures in him he was certain would sooner rather than later catapult him out of the landscape of his childhood, eastward, through this city.

"Let's go to the cathedral," Cheryl said. There it was on its hilltop, long and gray, its twin towers acknowledging the bleak February sunshine. There was no snow in Exeter. There never was. Instead they found crocuses, even daffodils in bud.

"Why?" Luke asked. "Do you want reassurance?"

Cheryl sighed. "I said it would be difficult with you. I'm a fool."

He laughed. "We'll go to the cathedral. Driver!" He tapped Adam on the shoulder. "Cathedral Yard, and step on it."

"South Street traffic lights," said Adam. "If not, you can make your own way down from E deck of the multi-story car park." They opted for the traffic lights. "We'll be in Tinley's," he said when they stopped. "About half past four. Be good."

Inside there was a surprising readjustment between what he remembered and what was actually there.

Instead of the expected silence and everlasting peace there was a perpetual rustling whisper, there was the reverberating confused echoes of voices and feet. It was lovingly looked after, as if it all still had point, but it relied for existence on the tramping of tourists' shoes, their needed aesthetic experiences gratefully acknowledged in postcards, guide books, putting money in the collection box. It was wider and longer than his memory was ever capable of suggesting. Lines of columns soared, grace on the surface of massive solidity; then the huge stone spines, the tree branches of the vault, which met and touched at the zenith, like kisses. But the enormous urge to lift the thing off the ground that all this symbolized, this need to fly toward Heaven, failed. It was a great box enclosing people in the chains of ritual, asserting will and authority. Thou shalt not . . .

It should have no roof. It should float up and up and up for ever. Perhaps in the war, when parts of it lay in a jumbled heap of meaningless rubble, that May night long before he was born, when Nazi bombs had shown that it would not last for ever, perhaps then it had looked at its most impressive, open to sky and wind. The miracle of its west window! The delicacy and strength of all that feeling in stone, flames and roses twisting and struggling! But it was frozen, locked, dead. Wasn't it all a vast mausoleum, a glorification of death, a sort of spitting on life? Everywhere sculptures, pictures, reliefs, words on brass plaques or carved on marble, praised death. The pale sunlight only emphasized it the more. Thomas à Becket, up in the vault, upside down, was kneeling resignedly, hands raised in gentle benediction, while the four knights butchered him. He was gratefully welcoming death, lunatic believer in the certainty of a martyr's crown!

Luke knew there was nothing afterward. Nothing at all. He took comfort in the knowledge. Becket was mad. So were they all—Bishop Carey, Bishop Grandisson, Bishop de Stapeldon, Bishop Bronescombe, Sir John and Lady Doderidge, Matthew Godwin, aged seventeen years and five months, "young, pious and gentle." A year younger than he, Luke, was. What had he known of life and loving? "A genius, bachelor of music, very worthy and very learned, master of the music in Canterbury and Exeter cathedrals." Why should all this dying be recorded? There should instead be sculptures everywhere of children playing, lovers making love; all the carvings Keats saw on the urn.

The organ started playing. There was a sudden indrawn rush of breath as it gathered itself together, then the loud piercing chord of G Minor, filling the whole building. The Bach *Fantasia* and Fugue! Now he could experience its full power, unrestrained by the inefficient little box of his loudspeaker at home, the scratches on the record's surface, the prickling of static electricity. The whole building shuddered. It would this time come crashing down on top of him. It was he who was shuddering, taken up totally against his will by the emotions of it, the diapason closing full in man . . .

"What is it?" Cheryl was shaking his arm.

"Nothing. Grandmother's footsteps. God's playing them."

"What?"

"Ssh. Listen." He took her arm and they walked up the center of the nave, feet in time to the music. "We're going down. Down. Like the steps at the deep end of a swimming pool. You think it's going to drown us, drown everything!"

"Luke!" She pulled her arm free, and stopped.

> *"Thou shalt remain, in midst of other woe*
> *Than ours, a friend to man, to whom thou say'st,*
> *'Beauty is truth, truth beauty,'—that is all*
> *Ye know on earth, and all ye need to know."*

"Luke! People are staring at you! At us!"

"I don't care!"

"You're shaking. Have you gone off your head?"

"No."

"What's the matter with you?"

"Nothing." He relaxed and smiled, held out his hand to her. They walked into the north transept and out of the door into the cold wind and thin sun, past the colorless statue of Richard Hooker, the art shop, the Clarence Hotel. And Jaeger's, where Mrs. Stephens, Elaine's mother, worked. Pigeons were flapping, people walking. The noise of cars, muted, on High Street behind these shops, accelerating as the lights changed.

"I think for a moment you were mad," she said.

"Not mad. Moved. I hate being moved in that way. Music does it more than anything else. I resist it and resist it, it seems so weak-willed. Then it just wells up and drowns me."

"I don't understand."

"Perhaps if I knew more about music it wouldn't happen."

"Why?"

"Familiarity breeds contempt." He wiped his sleeve across his eyes and nose.

"But you do know a lot about music."

"Not enough. I never learned to play the piano. We couldn't afford the lessons. I never learned any instrument at school. That was sheer cussedness on my part, I think. If I had, I could get my degree in music. Stupid. I've got perfect pitch. What a waste!"

"What's perfect pitch?"

"I can tell what key the music's in."

"Does that help?"

"I don't know. But they've all got different characters, different voices. C Major, the natural key. Ordinary life. Oh . . . forget it. Why are we always talking about me?"

"Because you're one hundred percent self-centered."

"I'm sorry."

"It's all right. I know what I'm letting myself in for."

Angie cooked a dinner of shepherd's pie and cabbage. It wasn't as good as Dad or Luke would have made it. But both of them caught Adam's eye and were silent. Dad, perversely, ate it all, unlike yesterday. Only Cheryl looked unconcerned.

"Had a good afternoon, Dad?" Adam asked.

"The entire racing program was canceled. Even the weather stops you winning a bit of money nowadays."

"Or losing it."

"Some film on TV I saw during the war . . . Load of rubbish, with Deanna Durbin."

"What was it called?"

"I can't remember. It's going to snow again, I think."

"Hope not. We've got to go back to Manchester tomorrow."

In Exeter they had forgotten the snow. But when they had driven out of the protection of the city they were reminded of it; the snow was thin on the first fields with the grass breaking up the shroud into mottled white and green furrows, and at the roadside it was gray from traffic exhaust or black with spots of oil. Soon it became an even white, suffocating everything. There was a wan pink sunset in Cornwall, menaced by massive gray clouds, one just hovering over the sun, then slowly sliding down over it, killing it.

Adam and Angie left soon after supper. They did not mention where they were going, though Adam said they would not be late—in time, anyway, for Luke to drive Cheryl home. When Cheryl was for a moment out of the room, Dad leaned across the table and said, "I like that girl. She's got class."

"That's not why I like her," said Luke.

"She's all right."

"I saw. You couldn't take your eyes off her, could you, Dad? There's a bit of life in you yet. Sly old critter."

"There's plenty of life in me. What do you mean?"

"I think you're better."

"Better?"

"You had a bad night last night. Have you forgotten?"

"Nothing to do with you."

"What are you up to this evening?"

"I thought I'd stay home and watch TV. There's the Black and White Minstrels, and a horror film later."

"I'd like you to go out."

His father grinned. "What's it worth?"

"I'll buy you a drink."

"That'll be the day."

"Come on, Dad."

"You needn't worry, son. I'm going down the Exeter about half seven. You can come down too, if you like."

"We might, later on."

"Why not? About ten o'clock. I'll see you in the Pretoria."

"I don't like the beer there."

"You drink it quick enough when I'm paying."

"I thought you said I was paying. Why not the Exeter Arms?"

"I'll be in the Pretoria just after ten. But I shan't expect you."

"Why not?"

"I'm not that silly."

When they were alone Luke said, "Don't mind Dad. All this."

"Why should I?" Cheryl asked. "What's wrong?"

"Nothing. It's different from your home."

"So?"

"It doesn't matter?"

"Of course not. It's you."

He smiled, relaxing. He pulled her toward him and kissed her hair. "Come upstairs," he whispered.

"Is it safe?"

"There'll be no one back for hours."

"I meant . . ."

"It will be all right. Come."

Three

I T was good?"
   "Real."
  "Real. Yes."
  "You, warm and heavy."
  "Once in a novel I read it said it was cars crashing
head on."
  "A warm loving sea. What was it for you?"
  "Not cars crashing. Not with this. A guy at school
once said it was having a bath with socks on."
  "You're disappointed."
  "It was beautiful. The most beautiful moments of
my life. Free. Really free at last. The most shining
thing that has ever happened in this world. Love—"
  "What?"
  "Will you go on the pill?"
  "I don't know."

"I'll come with you. It will be all right. We're both eighteen."

"I don't know."

"There's a family planning clinic here. I'll come. I'll talk to them."

"All right."

"You're beautiful. Your skin's a marvelous substance. Your mouth is most sweet. My fingertips on your body, my mouth, my tongue. You are altogether lovely."

"His belly is as bright ivory overlaid with sapphires. His legs are as pillars of marble, set upon sockets of fine gold."

"How do you know that?"

"I'm not all vacant in the head. I told you, I sometimes go to church."

"Ah. Have you just done wickedness, according to the church?"

"I love you."

"Did you say that to Tony?"

"Not fair."

"Did you sleep with him?"

"Yes. But it wasn't ever . . . it wasn't this. Do you mind?"

"Of course not." Luke leaned out of bed and lifted up the curtain. "Look. It's snowing. A wild white duststorm! A shower of white stars!"

"Come back. It's warm and dark in here."

He snuggled down. "Like life in the earth under the snow. Aren't these sheets, this eiderdown like a snow covering?"

"Warmer. Snow is like death I think. A shroud."

"We're soft furry creatures in a burrow under the snow."

"You are."

"What?"

"Your legs are. Dark hair. Nice."

"That's why you came to the squash courts so often."

"Fur forest. They're not pillars of marble. Long and warm and alive. All of them."

"Naughty."

"In the forest. Under the snow. Source of life."

"The sea. I'm a boat for your harbor. Warm and safe. Home."

"Dimples and hollows there, muscles of the abdomen. Firm. The curve of your arm there. Biceps."

"Flexors. Extensors."

"The edge of your shoulder-blade bone. The way it moves. It gives me a sense of your skeleton."

"Clavicle. Scapula. Head of humerus in socket of scapula. Why do you want the sense of my skeleton?"

"Because you can't be more inside than that. Bone and bone. Ultimate union."

"You're more poet than I thought."

"That's because you only think of you."

"I can't help it."

"You've beautiful hair. All boys should have long hair. Like a tent over my face."

"At school they once told me it was dirty. A bed of disease. They thought I had lice."

"And did you?"

"Of course not."

"What's to become of us?"

"Does it matter?"

"Not at the moment."

"At Easter I'm going away for three weeks. I'm working on a building site at Torquay. Almost everything I own I have to work for. Even my clothes. Come with me."

"How can I?"

"Easily."

"My parents wouldn't let me."

"My father wouldn't mind if you moved in here tomorrow."

"Mine would be horrified."

"I bet he knows where we are at this minute."

"You didn't tell him!"

"Don't be nuts."

"Extraordinary."

"Why?"

"Parents just aren't like that."

"Dad is."

"Perhaps that's why you're extraordinary."

"Am I?"

"Yes."

"Come to Torquay. You could find a job. We can find a room. Cost less than me living alone. Anyway I couldn't now. If you won't come I'll cancel the job."

"I'll see. Do you work during the school year?"

"Off and on. In Cornishes when they're busy. I've done a few nights in the pubs. Mostly I work at Browning's, you know, the garage on the Exeter road. At the pumps. Working with the customers."

"It's wrong. You shouldn't have to while you're still at school."

"Do you know, I was made in this bed."

"What do you mean?"

"This used to be my parents' bed. Dad couldn't bear sleeping in it after Mum died. He was going to chop it up for firewood. I persuaded him to swap with me."

"It doesn't seem right."

"What?"

"Making love in their bed."

"Why not? They aren't in it."

"The thought of my parents' . . . No. It's almost . . . sacrilegious."

"I think mine would like the idea. Anyway. It's only a bed."

"Were they very much in love?"

"Yes. It was a good marriage in every way."

"Sad."

"What? Mum's death? Well . . . you met Dad. He's just beating time. Waiting for death. Beating time. Adam and I . . . we're nothing to him, compared with Mum. I think you shouldn't ever be in love like they were. It's as if he'd had half of him hacked off. I often think of that image. Dad, minus a leg, an arm wrenched out, half his head and side missing. Because that is what has happened to him. You shouldn't ever love like that." His voice grew fierce. "It's terrifying!"

She stroked his face. "I'm beginning to understand you. Rough cheek."

"I'll never love like that."

"No. I don't suppose you will."

"Never lose the knowledge that it's finite. Not at any stage."

"As with us?"

"When I pass these exams—"

"*If* you pass—"

"With three grade 'A's and I go to Sussex in October, what will you do? Come with me?"

"I might."

"At this moment I think that would be the most sublime thing in the world, but will it really happen? What people will be by then, anyway?"

"You have it worked out. A nice little affair to pass the time. Give it six months at the most."

"That's sordid. I didn't mean that at all. You know I didn't. I just think there ought to be a sense of death in everything that's ever begun. I don't *mind* the idea. It just *is*. Adam said last night I just wanted the impossible conquest. Not true."

"You have it now. Perhaps he was right. We'll see."

"Made in this bed. One little seed, invisible to the naked eye. And now I'm as long as the bed. With millions of invisible seeds of my own.'

"Not making another life. A little Luke."

"No. Don't worry. You're wrong: it's eight months to October, not six."

"I can't see you as a father."

"Nor can I. Not by any stretch of the imagination. Luke, the married man. No."

"Thousands of boys have said that, and done the opposite. Dimples. Hollows."

"You're rousing me."

"A boat."

"You're greedy."

"Out of the harbor."

"In the harbor. I'm thinking of you all the time.

That's the difference. Other girls, trying to impress them how good I was."

"Running commentary. I know how good you are. Be quiet."

"I love you."

"I love you. Oh yes, I love you."

Saturday night at the Pretoria was crowded and smoky. Workers came with their wives. Light ales were served with the glass over the bottle. Babychams and a cherry on a stick. Factory workers were playing darts. Lots of red-faced young farmworkers out with their girl friends. It was a rowdy crowd. Dad was at the counter, staring into a half-empty glass of Guinness— it was ten past ten.

"All right?" he asked.

"You bet."

"Didn't expect you. Why I asked."

"Buying the old man a beer is as important to me as anything. You don't often ask me to."

"I'm calling for this. Sid!"

"Oh, no, you're not—"

"Sid! What do you want, Cheryl?"

"Sweet Martini, please."

"Sweet Martini, Sid. Luke?"

"Dad!"

"Give him a can of beer, Sid. He never touches anything else. And a Guinness for me. All right, son, you can buy one in a minute. We're not going just yet. Now go and find some seats while I bring these over."

They found three chairs round a table in a corner.

"Not your kind of pub, Cheryl," Luke said. "I'm sorry."

"How often do I have to say it doesn't matter?"

"It doesn't?"

"You've odd vulnerable places. I don't like them."

"I'd have thought they'd be welcome."

"Not yet. By October, maybe. But now I see you perfect."

"*Perfectus.* Latin for finished. *Ite, missa est.*'

"I meant created, made, a finished thing."

Dad joined them at the table. After he had swallowed half his Guinness in one mouthful, he put the glass down and asked, "Did you win your squash this morning?"

"No."

"So you're still human, then. For the moment. Who was the superman who walloped you?"

"Jack Crawley. You don't know him."

"Some relation of Crawley the bank man?"

"The elder son."

"Well I do know him then. In a manner of speaking."

"How?"

"I remember when he was a little kid about five. We was doing a job by their house. Laying paving stones, I think. Yes, a new foot walk."

"Well?"

"Well what?"

"Tell me about Jack when he was five."

"What for? There's nothing to tell."

"I'm interested. I want to know what you remember."

"Can't see why."

"Get on with it, Dad!"

"There's nothing to tell, I tell you! All right, if you want a completely boring story, and bore Cheryl as well, here it is. He was playing ball with some kids. Some ball game. Tennis ball. He kicked it straight into where we was digging. His Dad backs the car down the drive, a big car, Ford V-Eight, I think. Yells the kid out for knocking that ball at us. Manners, proper behavior, that sort of thing. Jack bursts into tears, runs to Mrs. Crawley. She was standing on the drive. No. Bending down picking carnations. White carnations. She cuddles him, says it doesn't matter. Nothing to it, is there? But now the odd thing, why I remember. Mrs. Crawley comes down the drive—very much, you know . . . real lady. Real lady. Scissors and carnations in one hand, holding the kid by the other. And *she* shouts at the old man like nobody's business. Didn't matter we was there. What right had he got calling out the kid, she wanted to know. Really went for him. I don't mean bad language, that type don't . . . but, good as. Know what I mean? Well . . . he just turns pale, winds the window up, and drives off down to his bank."

"That's all?"

"That's all."

"Well, I find that very interesting, Dad. Very interesting."

"Why?"

"Helps to explain something about Jack, that's why."

"Bleeding intellectuals finding hidden meanings in all sorts of rubbish. Get to that bar, son, or Sid'll call time. I don't know what the world's coming to, I really don't. Sit here for five minutes with an empty glass, and your son sits here staring at it. Look at him, Cheryl! Sits there, just waiting for the old fool to get up on his feet and crawl up to that bar a second time . . ." He laughed, a very rare laugh of real enjoyment.

Luke picked up the glasses. He grabbed his father's arm, and said, "You're a silly old man. You know that?"

"Get out of it." He pushed Luke away. "Get on. I want to talk to Cheryl. Best-looking girl you or Adam ever brought home."

"Watch him, love," said Luke. "He may look old and well past it, but he acts with the speed of lightning."

"Love?"

"Yes, Dad." Luke looked at him, and went.

"What do you think of him, Cheryl? Or is that a crazy question?"

She looked shy. "A crazy question, Mr. Edwards."

"Harry. If you're stopping for long, it's Harry. No friend of mine calls me Mr. Edwards."

"Harry."

"I'll tell you what I think of him. I'd give my life for him. I sometimes just have to look at him and I feel like . . . putty. I'd never let him know it, no, not in a thousand years. And I couldn't tell you why I feel like that, neither."

"I could."

He was amused. "No, girl. It's not that. All I know is you've got a good one in him."

"Where do you come from, Harry?"

"No marks, girl, for guessing that."

"I meant really, how did you come to live in this place?"

"Evacuated in 1939. We used to live off the Old Kent Road. Born and bred there. It was a good place. Yes . . . evacuated thirty-nine; my old man was killed at Alamein. He was thirty-six years of age. I was thirteen when war broke out, was sent down here. Never saw him again. I stayed here. Never went home, apart from when I was called up. The old house was pulled down, years back. There's a supermarket on that corner now, so I'm told. I've a sister who still lives up there, in New Cross Road. Runs a fish-and-chips shop."

Luke returned. "Big question for you, Dad." He sat down and sipped his pint. "Wits about you, Dad. Think hard. Do you think we're the prisoners of what our parents make us?"

"You and your silly games. Leave me out of it. Who took the top off this Guinness?"

"No one. It's all there. Serious question, Dad. Luke wants an answer."

"I don't know what you're on about."

"Something Jack Crawley said this morning."

"Well, he'd be a prisoner of his parents all right. Blimey! That setup."

"Tell us, tell us."

"Wouldn't you be? Big house, two cars, golf club. All that position to keep up. He'll have to marry some nice girl, same kind of money. Beg pardon, Cheryl. But he'd be forced to, wouldn't he, your John, what's-'is-name, Jack? Couldn't hang around with any old Jane, could he? Daddy wouldn't like it. He'd be a prisoner, all right."

"Ah."

"What do you mean, ah?"

"Nothing. Nothing. Nothing."

"Last thing you can complain about is being a prisoner of anything."

"Why not?"

"Come off it, son. You've been allowed to do more or less exactly what you pleased. More than most. I won't say more than's good for you. You've had to grow up more quickly than most, not having a mother. I don't know how parents affect their kids. I've always wanted the best for you. I've tried to give you that."

"I wonder if that freedom really is good for one."

"Look. By the time you were fifteen you were already older than most kids of your age. You're eighteen now. That's a man nowadays. You make your own decisions. Not for me to interfere. Anyway, most things you do are the right ones, and Adam too. Nowadays, anyway, since that Woolworth's lark I haven't had cause to interfere. I don't know what you're on about. You wanted a record player; I bought you one. You wanted to go out with girls; you went out with girls. Learn to drive; Adam taught you. You wanted to study; I didn't take you away and send you out to work. Could have used the money. I needn't tell you that."

"I just want to know how much I'm like you."

"Not much, boy. You've got brains. You'll lead a very different life. You already do."

"I think we're pretty alike, when all's done."

"I grew up quick like you, that's so. My old man trod on a mine in the desert when I was the same age as when your mum died."

"My mum. Your wife, Dad, please. Fran."

"When I was your age, Luke, I was on the Normandy beaches. D-Day. Grew up pretty quick there, or I wouldn't be here to tell you. You wouldn't exist."

"Complete shambles it was, every story you've told. Like Dad's Army. Eighteen. I can't imagine it."

"No kid ever can."

"And mademoiselle from Armentières waiting for you wrapped in the Bayeux tapestry, was she?"

"You mind your own business."

"Why?"

"I don't ask what tomcatting about you get up to, do I?"

"No. I'd probably tell you if you did ask, though. That's the difference."

"That sort of thing's private, son."

"Barriers. Barriers."

"There were a few French Janes, I suppose, now I come to think of it."

"Ah!"

"Well, what do you think? A lad of eighteen let loose in France."

"Very immoral, the French."

"Only thanking the liberators, in a manner of speaking."

"Very grateful, I'm sure. How many Norman brothers do I have?"

"That's none of your business, son." He meant it.

"Sorry, Dad. Sorry. The joke sort of slipped out of my hand. Sorry."

"All right. Don't go on about it. My glass is empty."

"I bought the last one. Anyway Sid's already called time. If you want one you'd better ask him. You know him better than I do."

"Do you want one? Cheryl?"

"No more, thanks. No more."

"I'll just get a couple of bottles to take home." He went up to the counter.

Luke took Cheryl's hand. He smiled. "Don't mind all the family stuff. That's Dad. Left you out of the conversation completely. Sorry."

"Mind?" She raised her fists and pretended to hit him. "You're out of *your* mind, Luke. I think he's great!"

"Funny old character, salt of the earth, that sort of thing?"

"No, no, no! I mean the two of you together. You really do communicate!"

Luke shook his head. "It's not so."

"If you can't see that, you're not half as intelligent as I thought."

"Tonight . . . that's something very unusual. It happens once in a blue moon. What sets if off I don't know."

"Perhaps us. There being the two of us."

"He approves. That's why."

"I don't know what more you want. You two . . . I can't think of any father and child who get on better. What more do you want?"

"Everything. Nothing less than everything."

"You're like a baby, crying for his mother. Must have her undivided attention."

"Yes, love. That is just what I am doing."

"Luke! I didn't mean . . . I'm sorry."

"I know. Just a manner of speaking, as Dad would say."

The snow whirled and fluttered under the street lamps, curves and parabolas, the wind, not so cold now, sometimes gusting it upward into their eyes just an inch before the flakes should have touched pavement or fences. It was less slippery underfoot. Their shoes could crush the surface into water. It was wet, clinging snow that dissolved on glass shop fronts in tears and streaks. At each drain in the gutter there was the sound of subterranean running water. Luke threw a snowball high into the air, over a street lamp onto someone's front door. His father threw one at him, a direct hit on the neck.

"A triumph for long hair," said Luke. "It might have gone down, slither-slither, ice-cold, down my skin. Didn't work. Yah!"

"You need cooling off."

"It's lovely stuff. Frozen sea spray."

"Not when you have to shovel it it's not. Ten minutes' work with it and you'd soon be on your back."

"Sob sob," said Luke, imitating a violin.

Dad threw another snowball, and soon all three of them were scooping it up, a real kids' snowfight all the way home, yelling, screaming for help, running. At the door of the house Luke turned and saw his father flat on his face.

"I can manage," he panted, as Luke helped him up. "Bit winded. That's all."

"What happened?"

"Slipped. What do you think!"

"Are you all right?"

" 'Course I'm all right. Unlock that door and let's get in."

"Bottles intact?"

"I made sure I didn't fall on them!"

"You'd rather break your knee than a bottle of beer!"

"Wouldn't you?"

Adam and Angie had not yet returned. Luke made cocoa for himself and Cheryl while she buttered biscuits and cut cheese. Dad changed into his slippers, knocked the top off one of his bottles and drank from it, and put his feet up on the sitting-room sofa. Luke lay full length on the floor in front of the electric fire, his head on Cheryl's lap. Cheryl knelt, braiding and unbraiding his hair.

"You should go to bed," Luke said to his father.

"What for?"

"You're old."

"And you two want the sofa. I know. What are you, rabbits?"

"Rabbits?" He raised eyebrows in mock incomprehension.

"You've had the run of this house all evening. What more do you want?"

"You never know what is enough unless you know what is more than enough. Why rabbits? Why not humans?"

"Forget it. I'm not going anyway. I want to talk to Cheryl. You managed to keep her out of the conversation all the time in the pub."

"I'm a born listener," said Cheryl.

"You'll have to be with him."

"I'm not saying a word," said Luke. "Not while she's playing with my hair. I like it."

"I know your father," said Dad. "Did some work up there once."

"Now we'll hear what your parents did to you when you were five."

"About eight years back, before I went on the roads. Bricklaying I was then. Did a wall in your garden."

"I remember," said Cheryl. "You told me off for moving one of the bricks. You'd just cemented it. You frightened me! A big rough man."

"What's he like, your father?" Luke asked. "I haven't ever seen him. Does he belong to the golf club, and things like that?"

"No. He's rather . . . withdrawn. The farm's very isolated up there. The frontier, he calls it. He thinks he's fighting the moor all the time, and the weather. He reads, listens to music, like you, when he has time. But he's not easy to talk to. Polite. Reserved. English."

"He wouldn't take kindly, then, to a working-class slob like me."

"Mmm. I think he would. He likes an argument. Picking brains."

"He was a fair-enough employer," said Dad.

"But we can't talk, not the way you two talk."

"You don't want to," said Luke. "We don't get all that far."

"I mean we have talked, yes, about the things you've been talking about this evening. You know, what was it like when you were young and so on. But I couldn't make jokes about sex, like you two. Or be so personal. Home is all a bit abstract. A bit formal.

"We don't have your warmth," said Cheryl. "In fact you make us seem a little . . . lifeless. I'm just beginning to realize what families should be about."

"That's stupid, Cheryl," said Dad. "You don't want to be like us. Most of the time we have awful fights. Hardly see each other one week to the next, except at mealtimes. Who'd want to see him, anyway?"

"We were showing off," said Luke, quietly. "Trying to impress you, that's all."

"You thank your stars, Cheryl, you've still got a mother. Home without women—that's no kind of a home."

"Love." Luke sat up and put his arms around her. "You're upset."

"I'm not."

"Don't. It makes you look even more beautiful. But please don't."

"I've just realized what you've done."

"What?"

"If this does end . . . you sort of put a date on it, didn't you? October. If I lose you, I have much less to go back to than I had before." He kissed her. "Luke, don't leave me."

"No . . . no." He kissed her again, rather uncertainly. "We'll survive. You'll see."

"Don't mind me," said his father. "I'm not even here for the beer."

"I'm sorry," said Cheryl, standing up. "That was silly of me."

"It was not," said Luke. "Old man, go to bed."

"Not so much of the old." The key turned in the lock. "Here, Luke." He leaned forward, whispering loudly. "I meant to ask you. What do you think of this Angie?"

"Not now, Dad. Have some tact." Their voices were already in the hall.

"She can't cook. Never says a word. Are they really serious?"

"I think they'll be getting married, quite soon."

"What! And I thought Adam had sense. Silly fool!"

Adam put his head around the door. "Angie's got a headache. She's gone up to bed. All right?"

"Yes, yes."

"The car's all yours, Lu."

"Thanks, Adam. Come on, Cheryl, let's be going."

"I'm off to bed, as well," said his father. He took the unopened bottle with him.

"Good idea, Dad," said Adam. "You stewed yourself unconscious last night. And you weighed a million tons."

"Sweet dreams," Dad said from the top of the stairs. "Be happy."

The snow under the tires sounded quite different. It splashed and hissed, turning to slush. It was still falling into the cones of light thrown by the street lamps, hurtling into the car's headlights and windshield. It was no longer hard little diamonds or crisp stars. There was rain in it. And the icicles on gutters dripped. The car tracks and footprints were gray, like pond ice melting, a thinness of water superimposed on them. The moor gate was wet. There was no difficulty in driving up to the farm.

"Are you coming in?" Cheryl asked.

"No, not now."

"Tomorrow, then."

"I'll come up as soon as I can. If Adam will let me have the car. He's going back tomorrow afternoon, so it's the last time I can have it."

"He's good about letting you borrow it."

"He's a great kid."

"Kid!"

"Love . . . we must talk." He put his arms around her. "We can't live on any sort of pretense. I can't make some kind of vow that things won't end in October. We might be finished long before then anyway. Or we might have decided, yes, this is it, we'll go off and live together. We might even be married. We just can't think in any of those terms, though. Don't make plans. Let's play it by ear, can't we? All I know is I love you *now.* I can't believe anything else matters."

"I know. I know. There's no need to tell me. I knew months ago that the terms would always be yours. I was just being silly."

"It was yesterday morning you came out of that café with me. It seems . . . light-years away."

"It is. It is."

"Then eight months. Consider."

"Don't go on about it. I know."

"Kiss me."

"Your mouth is most sweet."

"Your tongue tastes of cocoa."

"Idiot. You have the most lovely teeth. All straight and white."

"You're altogether lovely."

"Shall I tell them about us? About today?"

"Your parents?"

"I must tell them I know the only perfect person in the world. And that they'd better get used to the idea."

"Yes. They will have to."

"Come as early as you can."

"Dream of me."

At half past seven Luke dressed, went downstairs and made a pot of tea. It was cold and damp in the house, and he shivered. The thaw had made little progress in the small hours, but now, in the early gray light, it was slowly gathering strength. Everywhere outside water dripped. A wedge of wet snow sliding off next door's roof whooshed through the air and sploshed onto the sideway. Luke took two cups into Adam's room. In each other's arms all night, they looked like babes in the wood under the white wrapping of sheets and bedspread; innocent children. Slow, even breathing. Looking at them now he was certain they would get married, maybe even before Adam finished his degree. Luke prodded him awake.

"Go away," Adam said, sleepily.

Luke grinned and took the third cup into his father. He was lying on his back, his mouth open. Something was wrong. Luke put the cup down on the chair beside the bed. Something was wrong. The second bottle of Guinness stood on the floor, opened, but untouched. Then he realized. There was no slow, even breathing. Nothing at all.

He pulled back the bedclothes and put his hand on his father's heart. Nothing. He put his ear to the chest. Then he shook him, quite hard.

"Adam!" He shouted. "Adam! Help! Quick!" All the while he looked at his father's face. It seemed ages before Adam appeared. He could hear the bed creak, voices grumbling, Adam pulling on his jeans.

"What's the matter?" he asked, crossly, when he came in. Luke pointed. Adam too felt for the heart, listened for it, shook him.

"He's dead." There was bewilderment in his voice, incredulity. "Am I still dreaming?"

"No," Luke whispered.

"Phone the doctor. I'll get dressed and get Angie up. Hurry."

Luke did as he was told, though he wondered for a second what need there could be for haste now that it was too late. He rushed out of the house without a coat and still in his bedroom slippers, stumbling and slithering in the melting snow. His feet were wet blocks of ice by the time he reached the phone booth at the end of the road. After he had spoken to the doctor, he dialed Cheryl's number. The phone rang and rang at the other end. Cheryl's mother answered.

"It's Luke. Can I speak to Cheryl, please?"

"It's a very unreasonable hour, isn't it?"

"It's urgent. Extremely urgent."

Cheryl came to the phone. "I'll tell Dad," she said. "I'll be down immediately."

"But—"

She hung up.

Back at home he found Angie making toast. Upstairs Adam was still standing by the bed.

"He must have died immediately after going to bed. This Guinness isn't touched, even. Why, I was still in the kitchen . . . and when you came in he must already have . . ."

Luke found he was holding his brother in his arms.

"Only you now," Adam whispered. "Orphans."

"He didn't love us enough!" Luke said, with great bitterness. "He couldn't wait to join her! We were nothing to him! Why?"

"Don't. It's not true."

Half an hour later Luke was staring at a piece of paper in his right hand. Name, age, etcetera. Cause of death: cardiac arrest. So that was it. All that man just words on a piece of paper. The death would have to be registered, the doctor had said, and explained the procedure. He was sympathetic enough, used of course to this sort of thing. He slipped quietly and tactfully away.

The two brothers were dazed, numbed. They walked from one room to another, not knowing what to do or what to say. Angie looked at them, too shocked to help. She washed the dishes, made beds, made coffee. Luke felt nothing. It was as if he were staring at himself from a great height, looking at a useless object, telling himself he ought to be feeling this or saying and doing that, but he was too battered to react at all. Adam found a can of beer in the kitchen. He drank from it, offered it to Luke. Luke refused. Outside the sound of bells from the parish church were calling people to the Sunday morning service.

"We must get in touch with Aunt Glad," said Adam.

"Yes."

"I don't even know if she has a phone. And I must phone Manchester. We obviously can't go back today."

"No."

"An undertaker. I don't know one. Do you? And the Council."

"The Council?"

"Yes. His employers. And . . . about the house."

"What about the house?"

"They will want it back."

"What happens to me?"

"I don't know . . . we must talk about it."

"I'll make up my own mind. I suppose."

"Luke. You couldn't stay here, could you?"

"No. I suppose not."

"We'll have to go through his things."

"No."

"We'll have to."

"He would hate that. He was a very private man. Just . . . burn them."

Adam stopped. It was not the time. Luke, he realized, was much more shocked than he was. It was to be expected.

Luke switched on the record player.

"What's this?" Adam asked.

"Elgar. The E Flat Symphony. The slow movement."

"No. Turn it off."

"You need it."

It began with a sigh, a half-finished phrase on soft

strings. Then solemn trombones—a funeral march. Slow marching feet. The coffin on its gun carriage. The theme sank into the bass, lost in the rising nobilmente song, a decent expression of public grief, what's due and right. Not deeply felt. Yet. The oboe, the fourth idea, was more the real Elgar—wayward, uncertain, the hollowness underneath. A wedding cake being gnawn by rats. The naturally melancholic man. Now a real sorrow. Surely Elgar never felt that for a playboy king? It's the blight man was born for. It's Luke you mourn for. The music said all knowledge is futile, and all action.

Dad's life, his death: utterly futile. Why didn't he love us? All those most beautiful words in English were here; threnody, melancholy, poignant, plangent. Plangent, plangent, plangent. A first division composer if ever there was one. Never in danger of relegation. Vaughan Williams might be promoted if he had a good center forward. Now they combined, the oboe song and the cortege underneath, with an anxious repeated flurry of strings like heartbeats. Heartbeats! Made of muted string chords that sobbed like the sea. More and more like the sea. Architecture is frozen music. The cathedral. Reverse the proposition: is music thawed stonework? It approximates to the condition of the sea. A warm loving sea.

Childhood. The edge of man's consciousness. Where we came from. To lose oneself in waves, to drown in warm waves. We brought nothing into this world, and it is certain we can carry nothing out. The sea shall give up her dead. Longing for those loving arms of childhood dimly recalled, maybe never had, a total union; never with parents, of course not, but don't we long to go back into them? Now it was wilder, quite unrestrained; the emotion rose in him like a wave. He fought it but it overwhelmed him, and a dark nameless shadow rose out of him and disappeared. So we beat on, boats against the current, borne back ceaselessly into the past. He had to write an essay on this by Tuesday. How could he now? Gentle spread string chord, vast, over all the octaves, plangent C Minor.

Adam sat on the sofa, stock-still. No sound at all but there were tears right down his unshaven face. Luke lifted the needle off, and smiled.

"My mourning is over," he said.

"You had no right to do that."

"What?"

"You dramatize everything. This . . . measuring standards, music. It's tasteless. You made me cry."

"Why not?"

"You didn't cry."

"How do you know what happens inside me?"

"I was going to tell Dad last night. Only he went upstairs so quickly. I thought, over a drink this lunchtime."

"You're getting married."

"Yes. We bought a ring in Samuel's yesterday."

There was silence, and Luke said flatly, "I'm glad."

"It's not the time now, is it?"

"Of course it is."

"Will you come?"

"Need you ask?"

"The registry office in Salford . . . I don't know when. That's something else to work out."

He stood up, and walked uncertainly out of the room. Luke thought he had never looked so broken.

A car drew up. It was Cheryl and her father. He was kind and thoughtful, unobtrusively taking things over. He remembered Harry Edwards with affection. Realizing quickly the extent of the shock and sensing the total inability of the two young men to cope with the situation, he spoke gently of the funeral, death grants, insurance policies. He stayed all morning, directing most of his attention to Adam, leaving Luke and Cheryl holding hands or sitting on the stairs whispering.

By lunchtime he had taken it upon himself to see to all the funeral arrangements. He roused Adam sufficiently to go out and telephone Manchester, and Aunt Glad in New Cross. He learned that there were no relations in the neighborhood, no really close friends. What would Luke do if the Council wanted the house back quickly? Luke had no idea. Find a room somewhere. He didn't want to lodge with anybody. He just needed a room of his own which he'd pay for—somehow. Mr. Wood looked at him and said nothing. He thought they should all return to the farm for Sunday lunch. Adam refused. He wanted to be alone with Angie. They'd go out in the car and eat in a pub somewhere on the moor. Mr. Wood insisted, but Adam was stubborn.

They all left, relieved to be in the open air, but knowing the body was still upstairs and that it could not

be escaped and they'd have to come back later. Luke
went to the farm. Mr. and Mrs. Wood were tact itself,
giving him beer and leaving him alone with Cheryl.
But the nice ordinary dinner plates, the silver cutlery
upset him curiously. The smell of roast beef and York-
shire pudding was nauseous. Mr. and Mrs. Wood
talked decent platitudes. How good that it was thawing. The snowdrops were late that year. In 1963,
they'd been cut off for days; Cheryl was only six then
. . . knives and forks clattered . . . Luke cut up his meat
unenthusiastically. He felt slightly faint. No, it wasn't
faintness. He put his knife and fork down. Cheryl was
watching him. He put his head in his hands and cried
like a child.

Strong arms lifted him up, guided him into the
living room. He lay on the couch. Cheryl stayed with
him. He was filled with anger, a blind unreasoning
rage, that he had been forced to reveal such weakness
in front of her parents.

In the afternoon they climbed up to Quintin's Man.
Mr. and Mrs. Wood had tried to dissuade him. He
needed rest, a sedative. He objected, almost rudely.
They held hands, or he helped her over the difficult
rocks and through the patches of snow. But they said
nothing. He simply wasn't there. The snow was thick
near the summit, and frozen, and once again his jeans
were soaked through. He did not realize it for some
time, until the sensation, by now annoyingly familiar,
of icy feet, broke into his consciousness. The mast still
had no flag. It was just an uplifted warning finger,
encased in ice. A thin chill wind blew through their

parkas and jeans. From this roof peak the land stretched away, flatly it seemed, as far as the sea. They could not see the sea, but there was a sense there of the edge of land, perceptible lightening in the gray overcast. The cloud was a low ceiling pressing down on them. The moor, where it was not grayish white from unmelted snow, or black where the fir forests of Fernworthy and Bellever fell away into the distance, was a uniformly dull brown. There was no sign of life, not even a horse. Uncolored counties, Luke thought.

"Luke," Cheryl began. "I know . . . but I'm still here."

"Yes."

"And I love you."

He looked away. "I don't know how to answer you."

"What do you mean?"

"I feel . . . nothing. At the moment. No love for you."

"Luke—"

"Not for myself nor anyone. I'm like this landscape. Shrunk. Dried up. Every dead thing."

"It will thaw." She looked as if she wanted to be kissed, and he did so, mechanically. Pale cold lips, rubbery. Nothing there.

"Adam's getting married. He was talking of emigrating to Australia. I'm alone."

"Yesterday—"

"Yesterday was light-years away. Just as the day before was light-years before that. I don't love you, Cheryl. It's finished."

"I'm not worried. It's just not so."

"You should be. I'll only bring you harm."

"I'm not listening."

"I'm afraid." He was playing with a stone covered in ice.

"What of?"

"That next time we're in bed . . ."

"What?"

"It will just be sex. It would be so simple, not giving oneself to anyone. Just enjoying the sensation. No strings attached." The ice from the stone was melting on his palm.

"That's just the symptom."

"What of?" He threw the stone at the mast.

"It's you who's afraid now you'll be left. If this ends, then . . . then there will be no one to love."

"I don't know. I've nothing to give you. Adam was right. It was the impossible conquest. Big Luke, you see, that's what I've got to keep on proving. Let's settle for that."

"No."

"You'll regret it."

"Stop hurting yourself. It isn't what you want at all."

"Isn't it?"

"Yesterday evening it wasn't."

"No. I was a different person then."

Once again he was standing in front of the fire in shirt and shorts talking to her mother. His jeans were drying in the kitchen. The hair of the hearthrug again was sensuous on his feet.

"I've seen you more often without trousers than with them," she said brightly. She gave him a cup of tea. Eternal tea, sugar—sympathy, sedation.

"I hope you like what you see," he said, absent-mindedly.

She was not used to this kind of answer. She looked at him a moment, then said, "Luke. I think you ought to stay here tonight. Tonight, at least, or for a few days. Cheryl wants it. My husband thinks you should."

"You've been very kind. I don't know why."

"Cheryl told me last night she'd spent the day with the only perfect boy in the whole world. We'd offer anyway . . . anyone would."

"I must go home. There's things to do. I must see Adam."

"Will you come back tonight, then? Will Adam and . . . er . . ."

"I don't think they would."

"You can't stay there. Not . . ."

"I'll come. Thank you."

Cheryl's father drove him back to the house, and they agreed that Luke would walk up to the farm in the evening. A walk alone would do him good, he said. Adam was sitting cross-legged on the floor, a large pile of papers in front of him. "His things," he explained. "It's got to be done, Luke." He handed Luke a document of stiff paper. "He had insurance on his life. Read it."

"Not interested."

"Luke! Tell me, how do you think you're going to live now? Okay, you get to the university, you'll have a scholarship. It's pitiful, yes, but it's something. But for the next six months!"

"I'm not leaving school. I'm not missing my exams. I'll scrounge meals, sleep on anybody's floor rather than leave school now."

"You won't have to. That policy I think is worth about four hundred pounds. There's some other little insurance. Two pence, three pence a week things. Not much, but something. You could even have enough to buy yourself an old car."

Luke read it. "When we've split it, there won't."

"Split it?"

"It looks like something, yes. But hardly a car."

"I'm not touching it. It's yours."

"Don't be a crazy fool."

"I have a grant. I can just about live on it, if I work every vacation. You have nothing for right now."

"Fifty-fifty."

"No."

"Adam, don't humiliate me!"

"I could hit you sometimes. Even though you're the bigger. I'm not touching it."

For the second time that day Luke hid his head in trembling hands and wept. Adam pretended to ignore him. He continued looking through the papers, but watched out of the corner of his eye.

"Old bills. He seems to have had a weakness for keeping lots of old bills. One garden spade, four and six. One cotton shirt, twenty-two shillings. A few photographs. Here they are, just married, outside the church."

"Let's see." There was a date—1954. They were almost unrecognizably young and their clothes so old-fashioned. That long dress. Wide trouser bottoms. The clothes were never designed to fit or show off the body.

"I should have told you. He's gone."

"What?"

"Dad. The undertaker's men came. A special favor, they said, it being Sunday. Mr. Wood arranged it this morning. The funeral's on Tuesday, provisionally."

"Provisionally?"

"If we register the death tomorrow morning."

"It all seems a great hurry."

"Mr. Wood made some phone calls."

"Where's Angie?"

"In the kitchen. There was lamb for dinner today, but we weren't here. I couldn't have eaten it, anyway."

"I haven't had a bite all day. And I couldn't now. I'm going back to the farm for the night. They wanted to know if you'd come too . . . they've been very good to us, Adam."

"No. We'll stay here."

"What are we going to do with all this furniture? Sell it?"

"It's worth nothing. Probably have to pay the Council to break it up."

"I might need some."

"Where will you keep it?"

"I'll need a bed, won't I? Somewhere to put my clothes. Knives, forks, plates. But I've got no four walls or a ceiling to put them under. What am I going to do, Adam?"

"I don't think the Council will throw you out on the street. Do you want to stay here?"

"No. On my own . . . no. I'd like to get out as soon as possible."

"Start looking for a room, then."

Luke lifted up some of the papers and scattered them. "Is this all a life is?" he asked. "When it comes to it, a heap of old bills and tattered photographs?" Adam said nothing. "The end of a family. Some kids are held back, some . . . have adulthood thrust upon them." He stood up. "I'll be off in a minute, then."

"Stay till we've eaten. I'll drive you back."

"The smell of it will make me sick. Flesh. Ugh."

"Are you going to walk?"

"Yes. I'll be back in the morning. I've an essay to write." Adam stretched out his hand. Luke held it. Large, practical, almost identical with his own. "Don't leave me, Adam." His five fingertips touched Adam's five.

"You mean . . . now?"

"No. Afterward." He put Adam's fingertips into his mouth.

"I'm more afraid you'll do that to me."

"No. You're the hard one."

Adam smiled. "You don't know me at all, Lu. Not at all."

He paused outside the Exeter Arms, wanting a drink, but decided not to go in. He would have to speak to his father's friends: "Where's Harry tonight?" Those questions could be answered tomorrow or the day after. He crossed the road and went into the Fountain. He felt light in the head after the beer; it was the lack of food all day.

As he walked up the road toward the moor he began to feel distinctly unwell. He thought he was going to be sick. The houses seemed to be spinning. The houses were far apart, hidden by gardens. He stopped and gripped a fence post to keep himself upright.

Everything started to whirl. He could hear footsteps, and the patter of an animal's paws. There was yellow in front of his eyes; he gasped for breath. His legs would no longer support him. He was falling, but he could not stop himself. He hit the pavement and passed out.

Four

I T was a dog. He could feel its tongue licking his face. Someone pulled him up.

"Luke Edwards!!" It was Jack Crawley. "What the devil's going on?"

"I fainted. I think."

"Come on. Back to the house. That's it. It's only a few yards. I was just taking the dog for a walk."

The lights were on. He could hear the voice of a newscaster on TV. Jack helped him up the stairs to the bathroom. Luke suddenly lurched away and put his head over the toilet. He was very sick.

"I can't think why," he gasped. "I haven't eaten all day." He was sick again.

"Go on," said Jack. "Don't worry. You'll feel better." Luke caught sight of his face in the mirror, pale as wax, blood trickling from a nasty gash on his forehead.

Jack bathed it. "There's some dirt," he said. His hands were gentle. "I think you'll live." Luke's head throbbed and his throat was parched, and he was sore in the stomach. Someone was standing in the doorway. It was Jack's friend, Kevin.

"Man!" he said. "What's happened?"

"He fainted," Jack answered. "I found him in the road." He dabbed the wound with iodine. Luke gripped the basin as the antiseptic stung into his flesh. "You're lucky. It's just above your eye." He unwrapped lint and bandages. "Have you been drinking?"

"Only a pint. I told you, I haven't eaten all day."

"Why not?"

"I . . . I'd rather not say."

They took him downstairs and sat him on the sofa where Adam and Angie had spent all Friday evening discussing their future. Kevin sprawled on the floor watching the news. He and Jack did not seem very happy, Luke thought, even though Kevin looked as if he owned the place. Where was the rest of the family?

"It's marred your face for a while," said Jack.

Kevin laughed. "Was it a beautiful face then?"

"I've seen worse."

Luke smiled and stood up. The room swayed. "I was on my way up to Cheryl Wood's."

"I'll drive you."

"You look a bit like a cake just out of the oven," said Kevin. "That bandage around your head. A cake in greaseproof paper."

"Where's the family?" Luke asked. "I thought you'd be back in Exeter by now."

"Mum and Dad have gone out for a drink. Owen's seeing Kate home."

"Jack, I should have told you before."

"What?"

"My old man died this morning."

"Man! So that's why! Luke . . . I . . ."

"I'm all right. I'm all right." He said it a third time, in almost a whisper, "I'm all right."

"What happened?"

"A heart attack."

Jack fiddled with the television. "I'm sorry." He could not find any important words.

"I'd decided not to mention it, but . . . Look, you're going back to Exeter tonight?"

"Yes."

"Will you phone me? At Cheryl's. We'll play squash again. Friday evening. I'll pulverize you. Then buy you a drink afterward. We'll go out, all of us, with Cheryl, I mean."

"Yes. Definitely. Sure, Luke."

Jack drove him to the farm. His head ached dully and he felt very tired. But he was surprised that he did not feel worse; despite his fall to the pavement, the cut was not very deep. Underneath the skin of his head he was lucky to have, he thought, some very hard insensitive bone.

He woke much later than usual. Mrs. Wood had insisted on his taking a sleeping pill. His head hurt and his mouth was dry and tasted rough, but he was hungry at last. Cheryl brought him breakfast on a tray, the first time since childhood illness he had eaten a meal in

bed. This household was soft and comfortable to him.
He decided to go along with it, letting it flow over him.
Outside the sun was shining and he could see branches
in the garden, a field which was green, for the snow
had all disappeared from it, and beyond the dark lines
of the fir plantation, murmuring incessantly, a soothing, healing sound. A horse neighed in the distance.
Otherwise it was quiet, totally cut off from his normal
world of houses and traffic. Cheryl stayed in his room
for most of the morning. They talked about Dad, and
joked, mostly nonsense about themselves and people
they knew. She sat by the bed, her head on the pillow
beside his, his arm around her, stroking her hair.
Their eyes were huge to each other, blurred and
fascinating; little warm drops of moisture from the
breath of their words formed on their faces. Their
mouths touched tongue and cheeks and hair. Why
did she not come in beside him? he asked. He was
thawing. Some of the love he had felt on Saturday
warmed in him.

Eventually she went downstairs to help her mother.
Adam came. "Never fail to fall on your feet," he said,
looking around the room. "The luxury! Does she sleep
next door? No, here, I suppose." He looked serious.
"They told me downstairs what had happened. How
do you feel?"

"Not too bad."

"I've sorted Dad's things out. You must come and
see what you want to keep. And I've been to the registrar."

"I'll be down later. I may be taking my own stuff
away."

"Why, where to? What's the hurry? . . . You're not moving in here?"

"Possibly."

"Gadzooks. I don't know how you do it."

"It's just an idea. Cheryl's, in fact. I think she may be talking to her parents about it now."

"That will cause problems, won't it?"

"Yes. Nice ones."

"You watch yourself."

"I always do."

"Well, while you've been feathering your own nest I've been busy. The funeral is tomorrow. At Exeter crematorium. Three o'clock. Angie and I are leaving about two. You'll come with us? Will Cheryl come?"

"I haven't asked her. But I'll go with you, of course. Why do you ask? How else do you think I'll get there?"

"This is the death certificate." He gave Luke a long slip of paper.

Certified copy of an entry of death, pursuant to the Births and Deaths Registration Act 1953. Registration District, Devon West. 1975. Death in the Sub-district of Ockment in the County of Devon. No. 171. When and where died: Twenty-fourth February 1975, 23, Meath Road. Name and surname: Henry Luke Edwards. Sex: male. Age: 48 years. Occupation: Foreman, Urban District Council. Cause of death: Cardiac arrest. Signature, description and residence of informant: Adam Henry Edwards, son. 3, Waverley Street, Moss Side, Manchester. When registered: twenty-fifth February, 1975. Signature of Registrar: J. Stammers, registrar.

He handed it back and lay down, staring at the ceiling. What was it he said last night? Was this all a life was, a heap of old bills and tattered photographs? It was less, just a few official statistics. And there was still one further reduction to come. He remembered that after his mother's death he had searched in the *Encyclopaedia Britannica* in the school for the section, Cremation: The Burning of Human Corpses. One sentence was forever branded on his mind: "the type of furnace in general use is on the reverberatory principle, the body being consumed in a separate chamber heated to over two thousand degrees by a coke fire." He turned over and faced the wall.

"How are you?" Adam asked.

"The same."

"I don't mean your head."

"I know. You?"

"Yes."

"He willed it. It was deliberate."

"Luke, he loved us."

"He did not. He did not."

"I love you."

"Do you? I don't know. Not anymore."

He got up for lunch, still very hungry. It was cold meat, but he felt none of the nausea he had experienced yesterday. It was obvious throughout the meal that something had been decided, and he was going to be told at whatever moment Mr. Wood thought appropriate. But nothing was said. The conversation revolved around lambing, and the shortage of fodder. Mrs. Wood was anxious about the state of his head. He should take the bandage off after lunch and see if his wound was healing. How strange they were, Luke thought, compared with his own family, how indirect. If Mr. Wood had been Harry, the subject would have been thrashed out between everybody concerned as soon as it had been thought of. These people seemed all the time to hide behind little patterns and rituals so that their thoughts and feelings could be properly ordered. Their words often concealed more than they communicated. It had a certain tidiness about it, he supposed, but it was not warm.

Mrs. Wood cleared the plates away and Cheryl followed her into the kitchen, leaving the door open. Mr. Wood knocked out his pipe against the fireplace and refilled it slowly from an old plastic pouch. Luke sat at the table, waiting.

"Luke. We have a suggestion to make to you. Think about it carefully. You don't have to answer yes or no at once; I'm sure it's too soon since . . . for you to make up your mind about the future. It's Cheryl's idea, and she's discussed it with me, and I've talked it over with Jill. We'd . . . well, we'd like you to think about staying here for a bit. It's up to you. You'd be very welcome." He looked out of the window toward the fir trees. Tall man, thinning hair, check shirt, old tweed sports jacket with leather patches on the elbows, curly pipe. He did not like making speeches, but invariably found himself doing so. He went on, as Luke said nothing, "Cheryl has no brothers or sisters. She's always been lonely. This farm's so remote . . . when she was a child she would fill the house with imaginary friends. She used to get very cross if we sat down in certain chairs. Said we were squashing them. It would do her the world of good to have a real friend here. Particularly since she's broken up with Tony. You have . . . well, what do you say?"

"I'm not really a friend."

"How do you mean?"

"I'm a boy."

"I don't see that it—"

"I love her. As much as I can understand that word."

Mr. Wood coughed, embarrassed. "Maybe, given time, you might . . ."

"I don't know how it would work. You knew my father. A very different family. I mean I've lived all my life in a Council house . . ."

"You'd get used to us."

"Would you get used to me? You wouldn't like my faults if you knew them."

"What are they?"

"Well . . . I put my feet up on the sofa. I drink beer straight out of the can." Mr. Wood laughed. "I'm not very punctual about meals; I'm used to cooking my own."

"It doesn't sound very serious. What are your virtues?"

"I'm not sure I have any. I don't smoke." Luke felt he was falling into the role of the young lead in a bad play, about to ask for the daughter's hand. "I don't get drunk. I shan't go out at night very much, at least not till after the exams." He stood up, and wandered about the room, ill at ease. "This is silly," he said. "This isn't the point at all."

"What is the point, then?"

Luke's heart beat uncomfortably. It would have to be said, now. It would upset these people terribly. They'd been so kind. But it would have to be said.

"Cheryl and I . . . oh, God, this is impossible."

"Go on."

It was on the tip of his tongue. But he hadn't the courage; he could not. "It won't be easy . . . sleeping under the same roof." He blushed.

Mr. Wood puffed on his pipe. "I know what you mean," he said. "But you can't do that, can you?" Luke was silent. "Come now."

"No."

"You're a curiously frank person."

"Am I?"

"I like that. Well, will you accept?"

"I've nowhere else. I mean, I really am grateful. But . . . yes, I will. Thank you."

Luke again felt drained of all emotion. It was not the same miserable coldness the shock of his father's death had given him; it was not a sense of being unhappy in any way—more a total exhaustion of the spirit. He had been through too many extremes too quickly. He felt weary, years older, an old man. In the clinic that evening he experienced no reaction, not even to the doctor's evident hostility. "You're very young," the man had said. "Do your parents know?" He wrote out the prescription carelessly, almost illegibly. "If you were under eighteen, I'd probably feel obliged to tell them." He dismissed them without a trace of a smile.

Cheryl was indignant. "He just thinks we're dirty

and promiscuous and dishonoring our families!" she flashed.

"It doesn't matter," Luke answered, dully. Nothing mattered. Isolated bits of things of people's lives, all meaningless.

He went home and packed his clothes, his few books, odds and ends. He talked with Adam in a listless sort of way. Adam was in the same mood, dead. Luke went for the last time into his father's bedroom. He wondered if he would feel some sense of his presence, if the mere fact of Dad's having slept there would have some significance. The room was empty, just a bedroom, like anybody else's. He looked for something of his father's he could keep, some memento. But he left without taking anything.

Back at the farm he took the bandage off his head. It still hurt a little, but the cut was healing. While the others watched television he stayed upstairs and wrote his essay on Elgar's Second Symphony. It was one of the worst he had ever written; Miss Wharam would not be at all pleased. It had been going to be one of his best. There was so much he wanted to say about Sir Edward; that he was a first-class composer even if most of the pundits thought he was not; that the expansiveness, the long, flowing lines, the flourish and bravura, the pomp and circumstance of the music was a deliberate masquerade to hide the depth of his real feelings, his awareness of the pointlessness of human effort, of death in the birth of things. But, just as the great man could not bring himself in the slow movement of the cello concerto to write the last chord, could scarcely even complete the shape of the movement's theme, so Luke wrote only a few half-hearted sentences about what Elgar meant to him, unable to recreate in himself the profundities the music had produced yesterday. He devoted a brief side and a bit to a factual analysis of the symphony's form, its expositions, developments and recapitulations, and left it at that.

"Who is it?"

"Quintin's man."

"Luke. You frightened me. Be quiet. They'll hear."

"Can I come in beside you?"

"Mmm."

"You're soft and warm. Two whole days and I haven't touched you like this. You're there. I can't believe it."

"Stop talking. They'll hear."

"Kiss me."

"You're beautiful. I do love you."

"I'm going to stay here all night."

"You love me again."

"Yes. I think so. I'm going to stay here all night, I said."

"Are you?"

"Every night. Nothing else matters."

"You can't."

"Why not?"

"Be reasonable."

"I am. They must find out. I nearly told your father, but I was a coward at the last second. I wish I hadn't been. It makes me feel cheap."

"There will be terrible trouble."

"I can't live here on false pretenses. I'd rather leave tomorrow."

"I'd come with you."

"Would you? We're both eighteen. They couldn't stop us."

"I wouldn't be very happy about it."

"No. I don't think I would. Why is there always such fuss? Our love-making is good. It's all we have."

"They might accept it. In time."

"It's not honest, waiting. We must tell them."

"How?"

"Let them find my bed in the morning, not slept in."

"I'm scared."

"I'm here, love. Don't be."

"Luke. It won't be good. Let's not."

"Why?"

"I'm nervous. Tomorrow, perhaps."

"All right. Let's just fall asleep in each other's arms. That's never happened to us before. And in the daylight you'll be there, all of you, lying against me."

"They must know this might happen. They must have thought about it when they asked you to stay."

"Don't talk. Let's just fall asleep."

"Put your arm around me . . . there."

"My face is touching yours. Dream of me."

Nothing was said at breakfast, though Luke thought her parents were quieter than usual. Mr. Wood went out to his jobs around the farm, and Mrs. Wood, after washing the dishes in complete silence, decided to continue with the painting she was currently working on.

"They know," Cheryl said. "My God, what will they think of me?"

"Yes. They're working out what they should do, I think."

"They hardly ever say anything in temper. Luke. Please go up and talk to Mum. It would help. I'm frightened."

"I'm frightened too."

"Please."

"All right. I'll try."

Mrs. Wood used an attic for her hobby. The windows looked out over the moor. It was a large, untidy room, with canvases and books scattered everywhere. She was concentrating on a half-finished still life; a white cup and three stones, yellow and oddly shaped, like frozen waves. It was a very cool picture.

"I wondered if you would come in," she said, not looking up.

"Did you?" He was tongue-tied, and his heart raced.

She put her brush down. "You didn't sleep in your room last night." It was a flat statement, not an accusation.

"No."

"I'm not a completely old-fashioned person. I don't think I am. When two people are really in love, I don't automatically assume they should wait till they're married. But . . . I'm disturbed." She wanted him to answer, but he was too embarrassed to say anything. He concentrated on the picture, afraid of her eyes. "I know you're both in love. At the moment. It's so obvious! A pleasure to see. Luke. How long have you known each other? You must realize it's a bit hard for us to accept, to put it mildly. Isn't it?"

"Nothing happened last night."

"Didn't it?" She looked disbelieving.

"No. We . . . not with knowing you were . . . it would have spoiled everything. But I stayed. Deliberately. It was the only way to tell you that . . . I tried to tell Mr. Wood yesterday, but . . . If you want me to go, I'll clear out. I can go back home for a bit."

"Would that help?"

"I . . . don't know."

"Is Cheryl . . . on the pill?"

"Yes."

"Since when?"

"Yesterday."

She drew in her breath sharply, a sound, for the first time, almost like anger. "You've got it all worked out very nicely for yourself."

"Please. Please. It isn't like that at all."

She looked at him a while in silence, then resumed her painting. "We can't stop you," she said. "And you've obviously banked heavily on that."

"It's not true!"

"I will say this. I wasn't sorry about Cheryl and Tony splitting up. I don't know why exactly. I don't think they ever felt very deeply about each other, perhaps. One of those romances that just ticks along because neither of them could think of anything better, I suppose. It was time it ended. When she told me about you, I was happy for her. Really happy. And you've made a very good impression on us. On both of us.

John was quite excited about the idea of your coming here. A boy around the house, he said . . . he's always been sad about not having a son. He wanted you to drop this idea of going to Torquay at Easter. He liked the thought of you working with him. There's timber to cut, and he can always do with someone to help with the cows. It's all hard work for one. But now . . ." She sighed.

"I'm sorry." Much against his will, she was making him feel mean and shabby. "Do you want me to go?"

Silence. "I don't know," she said, eventually. "I really don't know."

"I can't . . . stay here on false pretenses. Nothing happened last night, but . . . it did on Saturday. Didn't you think . . . when you were discussing whether to ask me . . . that . . . ?"

"Yes. And I did point out to John if you were both here under the same roof, it would be a great strain in that way. But he seemed to think you should both be able to manage."

"But—"

"I know it must sound improbable, to you, yes. I thought . . . yes, it might happen, in time . . . it might be the right thing or not; it would depend entirely on how your relationship grew. But . . ."

"What's to be done?"

"I suppose we shouldn't have asked you to stay in the first place."

This was a slap. He stumbled toward the door. "I'll go and pack my things," he said.

"Luke! . . . No."

"Then . . ."

"I'm not happy about it. Don't think that, Luke . . ."

"Yes?"

"Don't make her pregnant."

"Of course not." The whole conversation was suddenly very distasteful. She could not possibly, he knew, have been more reasonable. But he felt guilty, all the same, ashamed of what he had done; his body was no longer an innocent and beautiful thing, but a secret degraded object, ugly.

"There's something else you must do." She picked up her brush and dipped it into the paint. "You must talk to John. Now. Go and find him."

"I can't."

"Why not?"

"I'm terrified. I don't know what to say."

"It's the least you can do, isn't it?"

"Yes. But—"

"Go on, then. I warn you, he isn't easy to talk to. And he won't be as sympathetic as me."

"Can I take Cheryl?"

"No."

"I just . . . can't."

"Luke. I think you're adult. Not a child. Don't let me lose that opinion too. Go and talk to him."

"I'll try."

It was a great relief to drive away in the afternoon. But they were on their way to his father's funeral, and he hated himself for feeling that such an event could bring comfort and consolation. What would Harry think if he knew? It had indeed been a difficult conversation with Mr. Wood, the most difficult of his whole life. Somehow they had got through it without any irreparable damage being done. In time the hurt he had given her parents would mend. He would do his utmost to see that it did.

Aunt Glad had been unable to come down for the funeral. Luke was rather pleased. She was large and bosomy and never stopped talking, and would have demanded an attention he could not have given her. The two sons and their girls, a few colleagues from work, those half dozen regulars at the Exeter Arms—that was all. The day was bright and cold, just the same as his mother's funeral had been. The gold light shone through the chapel windows in the same squares. He watched the coffin slide slowly away, but he felt nothing. "The body is consumed in a separate chamber heated to over two thousand degrees by a coke fire." It was a fact, just like any other fact.

Afterward the two brothers said good-bye. Adam was returning to Manchester at once.

"It will be in the Easter holidays," Adam said. "You'll both come, I hope. Lu, will you be best man?"

Luke smiled, very grateful. "I'd not have forgiven you if you'd asked someone else."

"Whom else would I ask?"

"You must have dozens of friends."

"Maybe. But only one brother."

"Where can we stay?"

"With us. It's only a tiny studio apartment. It hasn't even got a bed! We just have a mattress on the floor. I can borrow another one, I think."

"We'll manage."

"Stay for a few days."

"We will. Then . . . Australia?"

Adam nodded. "When, or rather if, we graduate. May we?"

"Ridiculous even thinking of asking."

"See you, then, lover. Look after her."

"Don't worry."

"You wouldn't come with us?"

"No."

"Well . . ."

"Good-bye, Adam."

Vacation was over. They awakened early, took Prince out on the moor before breakfast; there was time for a short ride. Luke was anxious to learn. He had visions of galloping across the valley, but Cheryl insisted they went at a walking pace, with her holding Prince's bridle.

"This is the way to see things," he said. "I wonder why I've never tried it before. I shall practice every day before school."

"Pay more attention. You'll fall off."

The snow had disappeared almost entirely. There were just a few wet patches under rocks that had escaped the sun. It was probably still thick on the peaks, but they could not see that far. The sides of the valley were shrouded in fog. Wisps of mist floated up from the heather and dead bracken, like smoke. Above, the sun was trying to break through the thin covering and in an hour or two would do so; now it cast a diffuse golden light so that even the fog itself in places seemed golden. Sheep rose up in front of them and scuttled away. Their damp gray wool made them look like giant thistle heads. A lark sang, an endless effortless bubbling, like water trickling from a tap.

"He's happy," Luke observed.

"So are we. Aren't we?"

"My legs are sore." He slipped off the horse, and they walked on, holding hands. His large hand hid her small hand entirely, cupped over it perfectly.

"Last night . . . was just ordinary. Wasn't it? I couldn't help it."

"It wasn't Saturday. No."

"It's silly to think . . . it will be perfection, every time. I suppose . . . sex is, most times, an ordinary enjoyable activity like anything else."

"Don't get neurotic about it."

"I'm not. Seeing my clothes in the wardrobe with yours. I like that. As if we're growing into each other."

"I was quite wrong when I said you made our family seem lifeless. I regret that. They aren't inferior to yours. Not at all."

"No, they're not. What have they said to you?"

"Not much. We're all carrying on as if life were quite normal."

"So it is."

"You mean so it should be. No one else we know can be so lucky."

"It looks bright, doesn't it?"

"Yes."

"I can't see an end in October. I see, at this moment . . . Permanence."

"Perhaps."

They were back at the farm. Prince was shut in a field with the cows. As they went indoors the fog swirled apart for a moment, showing the sky, a brilliant cold blue.

Over breakfast they chattered about school. Cheryl's parents watched and listened. Luke had English first period, the Metaphysical poets, with Mr. Mendham. Cheryl wondered what new recipes Miss Franklin, the home-economics teacher, would have cooked up over vacation to occupy her girls. They would see each other in World Problems, fourth period, with old Mr. Masters.

"I only wanted to start a conversation with you," said Luke. "Do you remember I wrote that on your desk? Ages ago."

"And I crossed it out. Yes."

"The Old Man will say at assembly how much he hopes we all enjoyed vacation. A time for physical and spiritual recreation, he always says. He's right, isn't he! I must go and see him at recess."

"Why?"

"Tell him about my father."

"And where you're living now?"

"Yes. How do we get to school? I never thought to ask."

"Today you walk," said Mr. Wood. "Sometimes I drive you. Occasionally you can have the car on your own. Depends on what I'm doing. Today you walk."

"Come on," said Luke. "We'll be late."

After they had gone, silence. It seemed to surge back in on Mr. and Mrs. Wood almost like a thickness, oppressive, like the mist.

"Are you sad, Jill?" he asked, after some time had passed.

"Yes. No. I don't know."

"I thought you'd be much more upset."

"I thought so too. I don't know what I think. Everything's just turned upside down. I don't quite know where to start again."

"Did we make the right decision?"

"We didn't make any decision. They just put a pistol to our heads. I don't know. However, I can see what she sees in him, all right."

"What's that?"

"I can't put it in words."

"Big strong lad. Intelligent."

"More than that. Something alive about him."

"Alive? I don't understand."

"I wish . . ."

"What?"

"Nothing. I just wish. That's all."